THE DRAGON PRINCESS

Borgo Press Books by GERALD VERNER

The Dragon Princess: A Novel of Adventure

THE DRAGON PRINCESS

A NOVEL OF ADVENTURE

GERALD VERNER

THE BORGO PRESS
MMXI

THE DRAGON PRINCESS

FIRST BORGO PRESS EDITION

Published by Wildside Press LLC

www.wildsidebooks.com

THE DRAGON PRINCESS

CONTENTS

PROLOGUE

The woman in the glass coffin was completely naked.

She might have been dead except for the gentle rise and fall of her beautifully moulded breasts. Her hair, black with a sheen like highly polished ebony, framed a face that even in its immobility was as lovely as her slim body.

Her eyes were closed and her lips slightly parted, full, perfectly shaped lips, inviting a lover's kiss. The crystal coffin in which she lay, her head supported on a silken cushion, rested on a black marble dais, and was bathed in a soft pink light that poured down from a peculiar shaped tube that was fastened between two electrodes of a strange hued metal that stood at each end of the dais.

At a bench covered with electrical and chemical apparatus of unusual design that ran down the centre of a vast laboratory sat an aged Chinese. His wrinkled face was expressionless as he watched with rapt attention the needle on a dial in a complicated machine in front of him. The needle quivered slightly, as it moved back and forth between two red lines on the dial.

A door at one end of the white-painted room opened noiselessly and a Chinese girl glided into the strange apartment. She was dressed in a spotless white overall. She paused, looked at the figure of the ancient Chinaman sitting motionless and absorbed, and then moved silently and gracefully over to the glass coffin. With bowed head she looked down at the lovely figure bathed in the rosy glow of the electric discharge above her.

The needle on the dial in front of the watchful Chinaman quivered violently, swing down and then up until it touched the thin red line in the centre of the dial. Instantly the Chinese shot out a claw-like hand and pressed down a switch. The rosy discharge above the woman in the coffin faded and the tube became dull and lifeless.

The Chinese got up stiffly from his seat. He moved slowly and with the deliberation of great age over to the marble dais. Standing beside the Chinese girl he looked at the woman in the coffin. The white flesh of her perfect body seemed to have retained some of the rosy light from the electric discharge and glowed with a faint inner glow.

The Chinese nodded his head slowly. With an expressionless face he turned to the Chinese girl.

"The ancient wisdom of the East has again triumphed over the ravages of nature and the passage of time," he said. "Her Highness The Princess Yu-Malu remains as lovely as the Lotus bud."

As he spoke the long lashes that rested on the soft

cheeks of the woman in the glass coffin quivered. Her eyes opened slowly. Her Highness The Princess Yu-Malu, illegitimate daughter of a Mandarin of the Manchu dynasty, smiled.

* * * * * * *

The co-pilot of the big Trans-Atlantic plane came through from the night-deck and made his way alone the gangway to the galley.

"Hello?" A stewardess, a pretty blonde girl, very attractive in her smart uniform, smiled at him as she uttered the questioning greeting.

"Any coffee?" asked the co-pilot.

"I brought you a cup ten minutes ago...."

"I know. I've got a thirst."

She poured him a cup of coffee. As she was adding milk he stopped her.

"I'd rather have it black...."

"I see. Slight hangover, is it?"

He grinned.

"Just a little." He gulped the coffee and gave her back the empty cup. "I say, bit of a beauty chorus on board this trip, haven't we? I've never seen anything so lovely as the girl in number four on the left of the gangway...."

"That's Princess Yu-Malu."

"Royalty, eh?"

"Chinese."

"Doesn't look Chinese. Give her bed and breakfast any time."

The stewardess made a face at him.

"You'd do that for any girl!" she said.

"Not breakfast!" he retorted. "I reserve that for the specials. What are you doing tonight?"

"It wouldn't concern you."

"No harm in trying. Those three other girls are quite an eyeful, aren't they? Can't remember ever carrying so much seductiveness on one flight before."

"Have you noticed anything about them?" she asked.

"You mean the vital statistics?"

"I take it for granted you noticed those! I mean all three are exactly alike...."

"Triplets?"

"Perhaps—but they're not sitting together."

"Maybe they don't like each other. I'd better be getting back. Be seeing you!"

He walked back to the door leading to the flight deck. The three girls watched with a slight smile as he passed. Real honeys, he decided, but nothing to compare with Princess Yu-Malu. He'd never seen anything quite so lovely in his life. It was almost impossible to believe that she was Chinese.

As he paused by the door before passing on into the flight deck and looked at her, she smiled. It was such a transcendently beautiful smile, so subtly provocative that he felt his pulses thrilling to the promise she conveyed. Very softly, in a voice that held a slight husky note in its creamy softness, she said:

"Can you tell me where we are?"

He told her. She smiled her thanks and raised a long

slim hand to her hair. One of the three girls left her seat and moved quickly and gracefully down the gangway towards the door to the flight deck, reaching in the handbag slung from her shoulder. One of the other girls followed her swiftly. They reached the co-pilot as he opened the door, and pushed with him to the flight deck.

Yu-Malu was adjusting a miniature nose and mouthpiece and as the third girl left her seat she, too, was wearing a similar breathing filter.

There was a faint hissing sound and the passengers seemed to find breathing difficult. Some of them attempted to rise from their seats but quickly fell back—unconscious.

Princess Yu-Malu rose from where she was sitting and nodded her lovely head in approval. The nose and mouthpiece prevented her from feeling the effects of the poison which the girl had released into the cabin, The stewardess, coming from the galley, stumbled after a few steps, clutched at her throat, and collapsed in the gangway.

Yu-Malu signalled to her accomplice who came quickly in answer and opened the door to the flight deck. Princess Yu-Malu passed through.

The pilot and the co-pilot were lying senseless on the floor. In their places sat the two girls, still wearing the same type of nose and mouthpieces as Yu-Malu and the other girl.

Skilfully they manipulated the controls of the big plane, their delicate hands moving with the assured touch of experts.

The plane swung round in a wide circle as it altered course.

Princess Yu-Malu removed the nose and mouth-piece and laughed—a low, musical laugh that filled the cockpit with a sound like the pealing of little silver bells....

* * * * * * *

The plane came sweeping down from a clear sky towards a small island set in an expanse of blue green sea. As far as the eye could reach there was no other land in sight. The island was rocky, with long ranges of low hills topped by stunted trees, their sides covered with thick undergrowth. The waves creamed among the rocks that piled in rugged shapes along the coast-line. So far as could be seen the island was devoid of habitation of any kind—a desert thrusting up out of the surrounding sea.

But the plane continued to come down, smoothly and with perfect precision, making for a long, narrow valley between two rising hills. It was so narrow that it was almost invisible even from the plane but the girl at the controls never faltered. She brought the plane in a long glide down to a smooth runway at the bottom of the valley. It touched down as gently and easily as though it were making a normal landing at a commer-cial airport and taxied to a stop.

As it came to a halt, a section of the runway on which it was standing sank down slowly, like a giant lift, and the plane disappeared from view. As it did so a section of the runway slid into place, so perfectly fitting, that it would have been difficult to distinguish any break in the concrete.

The plane on its giant platform was carried down until it came to rest in a vast and brilliantly lit cavern. A number of Chinese, headed by the aged one, came forward and steps were wheeled to the exit door in the fuselage. The door was opened and Yu-Malu, a lovely figure in her perfectly fitting travelling costume, stepped regally down the steps. She was followed by the three girls who had helped her to hijack the plane.

The aged Chinese met her at the foot of the steps and bowed low.

"Welcome back, your Highness," he murmured. "Once again you have struck another blow for China against the West."

Yu-Malu smiled, a sweet and radiant smile.

"Another large consignment of gold, Sin Wu," she answered. "Arrange for it to be taken to the storage vault. And have the bodies of the crew and passengers disposed of in the usual way."

"It shall be attended to, your Highness," said the old man. "The vital essence, so essential to your continued well-being, will be extracted from each one and then the bodies will be disintegrated."

"That is well," replied Yu-Malu. "Our reserves of gold are now complete. Soon we shall be ready to strike a blow against the Western world that will make it realize that China is rising from the ashes of her long dead self to take her rightful place as a supreme power."

She moved gracefully away through the bowing ranks of her followers to a door at the end of the vast underground cavern, which led to her private apartments.

And behind her, at a respectful distance, went the three beautiful girls who were exactly alike.

CHAPTER ONE

In a large office in Whitehall a worried Treasury official paced restlessly up and down. As he walked he talked—jerkily—in sharp quick little sentences that tallied with the nervous state he was in.

"Vanished! Into thin air! No trace whatever! Incredible—absolutely incredible! Something's got to be done, Race. It's got to! The Prime Minister is shocked—shocked to the core."

Anthony Race, brown, lean, relaxed in contrast to the man who machine-gunned words at him as he drifted aimlessly about the comfortable room, remained silent.

"You're the Treasury's head security officer. Can't you do something?" went on the other with scarcely a pause. "It's not the first, you know. Oh, no, it's not the first. Gold has been disappearing in transit at an alarming rate! The total runs into many millions, countless millions. Where has it gone? Who's responsible? Eh? Eh? Why don't you say something? What's the good of just sitting there? Something's got to be done...."

"It's no good my talking for the sake of talking," broke in Race in a pleasantly deep voice in contrast to the high official's shrill, petulant tones.

"Is that all you can say?" The other stopped by the big desk and fingered an ornate lighter with nervous fingers. "I've got to report to the P.M. personally. What am I going to tell him, eh? That it's no good talking for the sake of talking? What d'you suppose he'll say to that?"

"Most of the things he usually says!" said Race. "A whole lot of rubbish that sounds good and means nothing!"

"That's all very well," grumbled the high official. "But we've got to have something concrete, practical, to report. Look here! Somebody has been stealing gold at an alarming rate. The drain can't continue. It's got serious. We've tried various means of transport—the only thing we haven't tried is a blasted submarine—and the result is always the same. There were eight security guards on this last plane. Took their places among the passengers. The whole damn lot, passengers, plane, the bloody lot—gone. Just like that!" He snapped his fingers.

"I'm not saying it isn't serious...."

"I shouldn't think you were! Serious!" He spluttered in his agitation to find suitable words and Race jumped in quickly.

"I know how serious it is. I've got Katrina following up a line that may lead somewhere...."

"Oh! What?"

The high official swung round sharply. His round, rather bovine face showed interest.

"Don't get all het up. There may be nothing in it, It's just a possibility...."

Race broke off as there was a tap at the door and, without waiting for an invitation, a girl came quickly into the office. She was a plain girl. Her hair was dressed severely back from her forehead and coiled into a bun at the nape of her neck. She wore shell-rimmed glasses and practically no makeup. Her clothes were smartly cut but lacked any touch of femininity.

"Hello Katrina," greeted Race. "What luck?"

"I think I've found something." She came over to the desk, opened a large handbag and took out some papers. "I followed up your suggestion. These are the passenger lists of the last three missing planes. She spread the papers out flat on the desk and Race and the high official crowded round her. "Look—do you see? There's one name that appears on all of them...."

"Yu-Malu!" breathed Race.

Katrina nodded.

"Significant, isn't it?" she said. "All the other people on those planes have never been heard of since...."

"But Yu-Malu has cropped up again every time...."

"Who is this Yu-Malu?" demanded the high official.

Race sighed. It was extraordinary, he thought, that officialdom should always be so ignorant.

"Princess Yu-Malu is of Chinese origin," he said.

"Actually very little has filtered out of that enigmatic country about her. But there have been rumours—rather strange rumours...."

"Foreigners!" The high official sniffed distastefully.

"Yu-Malu has been called the most beautiful woman in the world," Race went on, taking no notice of the interruption. "She is the illegitimate daughter of a Mandarin of the Manchu dynasty of Ch'ing. Her mother was an American beauty. She's immensely wealthy. Her grandfather was killed in the Boxer uprising and she inherited the accumulated fortunes of the Manchus...."

"You don't seriously suggest that this woman is responsible for this gold drain?" The high official's expression was incredulous.

"It's rather queer that she should have been a passenger on those planes, isn't it?" put in Katrina. "Whatever happened to the other people she must have survived..."

"Exactly." Race nodded. "She's known to hate everything connected with the Western world. In China they call her the Dragon Princess. Nothing has ever been actually proved against her but there have been rumours that quite a number of international disorders have been organised by her...."

"You think that all this gold has gone to China?" The high official looked aghast at the thought. "Good God! Steps must be taken at once. This—this woman must be stopped!"

"It's only an idea of mine that she is behind it...."

"Follow it up! You must do everything possible!"

"I shall require absolute authority...."

The high official made a sweeping gesture.

"I will see the P.M. You will be granted the fullest

possible powers. Every ministry will be instructed to cooperate. China! Whoever imagined that the so-called 'Yellow Peril' would crop up again...."

"China has always been an inscrutable country. Does anyone really know what goes on inside? Katrina, go along to the Foreign Office. Get hold of Mathews. He's an authority on China. Tell him I want to know everything that is known concerning Princess Yu-Malu. I doubt if he'll be able to tell you very much, but we might get hold of something useful."

Katrina nodded.

"Where do I contact you?" she asked.

"At the usual place. After six."

She nodded again, walked to the door and went out.

"I want to talk to you," said Race when the door had shut behind her. "Seriously. What I'm going to say is confidential. Sit down, please."

The high official opened his mouth to say something thought better of it, and dropped heavily into the chair behind his desk.

Anthony Race hitched his chair nearer. Dropping his voice he began to speak rapidly. As he continued the somewhat protuberant eyes of the high official grew more prominent.

* * * * * * *

The Princess Yu-Malu's beautiful golden-brown body slid through the cool, perfumed water of her luxurious swimming pool. It was a large pool, cunningly contrived by the skilful use of tropical plants and flowers to appear of a natural formation. A waterfall trickled over a shallow terrace of rocks, feeding the pool with a constant supply of clean fresh water, tapped from an underground spring and warmed artificially to a constant temperature a little above blood heat.

A fountain, spraying from a concealed jet in a pile of rocks in the centre of the oblong-shaped pool, splashed musically and supplied the delicate perfume that scented the water and hung in the air. Concealed lights shed a soft glow that resembled sunlight and the warm air was heated by invisible infra-red rays. At one end of this unusual and luxurious bathing pool was a strip of silver sand on which the water lapped gently and also on which had been set cushioned reclining chairs and swinging hammocks. Beyond this was a bar, presided over by a Chinese girl, and stocked with every known kind of drink and sweetmeat.

Yu-Malu spent much of the tune, when she was at home in her underground headquarters, in this delectable place. She found the atmosphere soothing and she was able to relax completely, sometimes alone and sometimes in the company of the beautiful girls whom she had recruited from all parts of the world to assist her in her campaign against the Western world.

She loved to be surrounded by water. She bathed and swam completely naked, revelling in the sensual caress of the water on her flesh. There was something elemental in her nature that responded to the soft touch of it on her body and she thrilled to its smooth ripples as she might to a lover's hand. Beneath her outward sophistication, Yu-Malu was pure pagan. She was a Moon-worshipper and the Feast of the Full Moon was always celebrated in the ancient tradition.

Her low, musical laugh floated over the clear blue water as she swam with swift and graceful strokes in a race with the three girls who had been her companions on the plane. Now, without the thin but perfectly made rubber masks that they had worn, they were no longer alike. But they were very lovely, each of a distinctive type. Yu-Malu numbered a great many of these girls among her retinue, all beautiful physically and all devoted with a fanatical devotion to their incredibly beautiful mistress. They were known as The Dragonflies, and they were distinguished by a number prefixed by the letter 'D'.

Like Yu-Malu, herself, they swam completely naked, and like her they seemed to revel in the touch of the water as it slid over their nude bodies.

For a long time they splashed and frolicked among the trailing flowers and foliage of the pool and then Yu-Malu decided that she had had enough.

Her attentive maid, waiting ready with a beautifully embroidered robe, slipped it on over the Princess's lovely body as she stepped daintily out of the water. Yu-Malu sank into one of the cushioned chairs.

"Bring me the telephone and some tea," she ordered. The maid bowed.

"Yes, your Highness," she murmured.

While she was gone to obey the order, Yu-Malu helped herself to a tiny cigarette, tipped with a rose petal, from a silver box of rare Chinese workmanship that stood on a low table beside her. The girl from the bar was at her side before she could put the cigarette between her lips and had flicked a lighter into flame. The Princess dipped the end of the little cigarette into the flame and acknowledged the service with an, inclination of her head. As she pursed her perfectly shaped lips and blew out the first stream of smoke, the maid returned with the telephone, trailing a long lead.

She put the instrument down on the low table, bowed again, and withdrew to fetch the tea.

Yu-Malu lifted the receiver and pressed one of the number of buttons on the base of the telephone.

"Can you come to the pool?" she asked. "I wish to speak with you, Sin Wu."

She replaced the receiver and leaned back in the chair. The three Dragonflies were still laughing and splashing in the pool and she watched them with an expressionless face until her tea was served to her in priceless Ming china.

She was sipping from the handleless cup in the Chinese fashion when the old man, feeble, but radiating a great dignity approached.

"Your Highness requires my presence?" he asked, lowering his head before her.

She nodded.

"Be seated, Sin Wu. You will drink a bowl of tea?"

"Thank you, no," he answered as he seated himself in a chair beside her. "I have but recently taken my tea. You are more beautiful than you have ever been, your Highness. The treatment does not fail. It acts on both the physical body and the mental capacity, rejuvenating both in the same degree. You are as lovely as a young girl—ageless as the moon and the stars."

"What is my age, Sin Wu?"

The Chinese spread his long, thin, wrinkled hands and gently shook his head.

"It is of little consequence," he said. "We are not like the West. We reverence and venerate age. Let it be sufficient that you will continue as you are now so long as you receive the periodic rejuvenation treatment, the secret of which was discovered in a monastery in Tibet by one of your illustrious ancestors."

"When I have achieved my object," said Yu-Malu, "when I have raised China to the leading power in the world, when I have completely subjugated the Western world and utterly destroyed its so-called civilization, then, Sin Wu, will I go to my rest in the grave of my ancestors."

"That is your destiny," replied the old man. "It was for that that you were called into the world. The members of the Triad have arrived."

"The meeting is for tonight. They have been well looked after?"

Sin Wu inclined his head.

"I have personally arranged for their comforts," he answered. "There are now sixty, a representative from each branch of the Hung Brotherhood..."

"It is as well so many are here," said Yu-Malu. "I have information of the greatest importance to give them."

"The time is at hand?" It was more a question than a statement.

"The Western peoples number three thousand and fifty millions. We number seven hundred millions. And yet we hold no power in the world. Our government states that we shall continue to fight against American Imperialism, and against Soviet Revisionism. I have something to offer China better than words." Her eyes glowed with the light of the fanatic. She rose to her feet, radiating an inner power that was like a tangible force. Sin Wu rose too, standing with bowed head and hands clasped across his breast.

"I am offering deeds!" cried the Dragon Princess. "The West will do well to heed, or it will be destroyed."

CHAPTER TWO

The room was lighted by concealed lights round the ceiling cornice. It was a huge room, long and appearing narrow because of its length.

There was no furniture in it except a polished table that ran down the centre for nearly the entire length, and chairs set at intervals along either side. At the head of the table was a dais, slightly raised above floor level, on which a chair of some black wood that looked like ebony but was not, stood on a thick mat. The arms of the chair and its twisted legs were beautifully carved in the semblance of dragons, an exquisite example of Chinese craftsmanship.

Each of the chairs that lined either side of the table was occupied—thirty on each side.

And the sixty occupants were all exactly alike.

In dress, in features, there was not a pin to choose between them. They might have been made in the same mould.

Seated in the carven chair, dressed in a low-cut evening gown that clung to her figure revealing every perfect and voluptuous curve, her lovely face inscrutable, Yu-Malu surveyed this weird scene through half-closed eyes. The subtle perfume which seemed to linger everywhere in her underground headquarters and which was distilled from a secret formula in the huge laboratories, permeated the air.

In a smaller chair at the foot of the long table sat, Sin Wu.

There was absolute silence, a silence that was heavy with expectancy. Yu-Malu leaned slightly forward, stretched out a rounded arm, and struck a small silver gong on the table in front of her.

As the musical note vibrated to silence, she rose to her feet. For a moment or two she let her eyes travel over the uncanny assembly, and then she began to speak. Her voice was low, with a cadence that was like the notes from a well-played violin. It filled the entire room so that all those present could hear every syllable without effort.

"Gentlemen of the Hung Brotherhood," she said, "I have called this meeting to inform you that our efforts on behalf of China are soon to show results. As you are already aware, we have over the past few years been acquiring a store of gold. Our strong room on the island is full."

A gentle murmur, like the whispering of a soft wind, went round the table as she paused.

"The Triad, the powerful secret society founded in the seventeenth century, of which you, gentlemen, form the Inner Circle, and who have been pleased to elect me as your Empress, may have wondered why we have collected this gold which, after all, although of considerable value, represents only a very small portion of that held by the Western and other countries. I am, gentlemen, about to tell you."

Again, as she paused, the wind swept round the table like the rustle of leaves.

"For a long time," continued Yu-Malu, "my scientists have been working on an invention that will strike a crippling blow against our enemies of the West. Give the signal, Sin Wu."

The aged Chinaman at the foot of the table reached out a claw-like hand and touched a button set in the polished surface of the table before him.

A concealed door in one wall of the long room slid back noiselessly. Three of the Dragonflies, wearing identical rubber masks and dressed exactly alike, wheeled in a large trolley on which rested a complicated apparatus of switches and dials, surmounted by something that looked like a miniature radar directional aerial.

The three girls brought the trolley to the bottom of the table so that it faced Yu-Malu and was visible to all those seated in the chairs.

"You have tested the machine?" asked the Dragon Princess.

One of the girls who appeared to be in charge bowed in the affirmative.

"It works perfectly," she said.

"And the range?"

"Five hundred yards, your Highness."

"That is sufficient for our purpose," said Yu-Malu.

She drew herself up to her full height and surveyed the strange gathering for a moment in silence. "This is my gift to China," she continued, and her eyes glinted with an inward glow, like the chatoyant eyes of a cat. "This, gentlemen, will *destroy* gold when the ray is turned on."

There was a murmur from the men round the table.

"It affects nothing else, but gold is reduced to a powdery grey ash." Her voice rose slightly. "Can you imagine, gentlemen, what effect this could have on the Western Peoples? Can you not realize what a tremendous power this will give to China? Now I can strike the first blow in my scheme to make China a leading force in the world. *The* leading force! The Western world, and all those countries who do not accept China, will be crushed—reduced to a powdery ash like their own gold."

* * * * * * *

"I don't," remarked Katrina, Anthony Race's assistant, "know why we should be wasting our time here."

She was sitting in the lounge of the Hotel Splendide in Monte Carlo, facing her employer. She looked as plainly efficient as usual, impeccably dressed but in a severe style that was slightly masculine. Amid the feminine beauty that surrounded her, clad in the latest Paris creations, she looked almost drab.

"We're not wasting time," said Race. He stubbed out his cigarette in an ashtray. "We're doing our job."

"I should have thought," retorted Katrina, "that any

security officer could keep an eye on Mark Walker. Oh, I know he's important but why did we have to drop the gold business and Yu-Malu? Surely that was just as important?"

"Apparently the powers that be thought otherwise," said Race. "I don't know what you're grumbling at. Here you are in Monte Carlo at the height of the season, staying in the best hotel and getting paid for it! Lots of girls would go purple with envy."

"Well, I'm not lots of girls, I'm me!"

"Walker is dynamite," Race continued. "A real dyed in the wool genius. A V.I.P. of the first water. If this new rocket fuel he's invented is all that he claims it will revolutionize space travel...."

"And weapons?"

Race shrugged his shoulders.

"And those, of course. Think how much cheaper it will make rockets of all kinds—and lighter, too. Since it's a cold fuel, relying on the mixture of certain chemicals to produce an enormous expansion of gases, it requires no ignition. The rocket can be constructed of thinner and less expensive metals...."

"I know all that," interrupted Katrina impatiently. "But why do we have to look after him while he's on vacation? It's an ordinary security job and has nothing to do with the Treasury...."

"Wrong. The Treasury have sunk an enormous amount of money in Walker's research work. They don't want some foreign power to swoop down and whisk Walker away. He's the white-headed boy. Hence us!"

"He certainly seems to be enjoying his holiday," said Katrina.

Race turned his head and followed the direction of her eyes. A well-built, good-looking man of about thirty had entered the lounge. He was accompanied by a very attractive girl and they were both laughing.

"Even scientists must have their love-life," said Race. "He's certainly got an eye for a good thing!"

"Perhaps you'd like to change places," said Katrina coldly.

"Apparently a good many of the men here would," retorted Race.

The eyes of the majority of the males swivelled round to follow Walker and his lovely companion as they strolled across the lounge and went into the bar.

But the sensation was mild compared with what was to follow. Heralded by an obsequious waiter, the Princess Yu-Malu entered the lounge.

The admiration that swept through that thronged place was almost audible, and there was justification for it.

Yu-Malu, a vision of loveliness that put to shade every other woman there, walked with the regal carriage of a queen to the reserved table to which the waiter conducted her, ignoring the stares and the whispers and the people who were responsible for them.

Seating herself with a graceful movement that few could have emulated, she took out a jewelled cigarette case and helped herself to one of her tiny, rose-petal tipped, cigarettes. With a matching lighter she lit the cigarette and blew a thin stream of smoke from her exquisitely shaped lips. Leaning back in her chair she let her eyes travel slowly, rather insolently, round the lounge.

Katrina, with slightly parted lips, turned to Race.

"Yu-Malu!" she breathed. "What's she doing here?"

"Walker," said Race. "She's risen to the bait."

"You mean that you expected her...?"

"I hoped."

"I'm beginning to understand."

"You didn't think we should be wasting our time over Walker if it wasn't that the big fish might bite?"

"Well, I did rather wonder."

"We'll have to keep doubly vigilant now she's here."

"What do you suppose she'll do?"

Race screwed up his face in a grimace that was intended to indicate uncertainty.

"I think she'll try and get hold of him," he said. "She wants that formula for China. It was allowed to leak out that Walker would be spending his vacation here..."

"I suppose you saw to that?"

"Of course."

He took out his cigarette case, offered it to Katrina and took a cigarette himself. When they were both alight he continued:

"I've collected a lot of information about Yu-Malu. She's a fanatic on the subject of China. Her ambition is to restore the glories of the Manchu dynasty. She's fabulously wealthy and she can command the implicit loyalty of her followers. What she says is law. She's utterly ruthless. Although men fall for her like skittles, she's as cold as the top of the Himalayan mountains and when anything like that is necessary for her plans she delegates the job to one of her innumerable female followers. These girls are all picked for their beauty, and they are quite prepared to suffer torture and even death for the Dragon Princess...."

"How do you know all this?" Katrina looked at him curiously.

"Odd bits and pieces that have trickled in over a long period. I've had my suspicions of Yu-Malu for a long time. My candid opinion is that she's our greatest danger. I've an idea that the Soviets think the same. She's no time for communism. She wants a despotic rule, with China, represented by herself, as the ruling nation. And she could succeed. She's got brains, a rare quality in the leaders of today She's also got imagination. The two combined have always been a force to be reckoned with."

He knocked the ash from his cigarette into the ashtray, Katrina looked across at the subject of their conversation.

Yu-Malu, perfectly at ease, and apparently completely oblivious of her surroundings, was crushing out the stub of her tiny cigarette. The light from the wall fitment above her head struck a green spark from a ring on her finger. It was a large ring set with a green stone of some kind. Katrina was too far away to see it plainly.

"Let's go into the bar and see what Walker and his girlfriend are up to," suggested Race. He got lazily to his feet and waited for Katrina to join him.

As they sauntered towards the entrance to the bar, Yu-Malu's eyes followed them.

* * * * * * *

Brian Gilmour, one of the routine security officers detailed to watch over the safety and well-being of Mark Walker, sat in a far corner of the Splendide bar and stared gloomily into his third pink gin. He was a thick-set, florid-faced, rather bovine looking man.

And he was bored.

Around him people were laughing and enjoying themselves but he would rather have been back in his small house in Potters Bar with his wife.

It was a hell of a life working for security, he thought. It might suit some people, but certainly not him. But it was a living and one couldn't pick and choose these days. Certainly Mark Walker seemed to be enjoying himself. He was smiling down into the upturned face of his beautiful companion who appeared to be enthralled at whatever it was he was telling her.

Gilmour had seen him pick her up on the previous day. At least it had been more of a pick-up on her part. An old dodge but in this case very well done. Sand in her eye! Gilmour was ready to bet that there had been nothing in her eye—except Mark Walker. He had been suspicious and doubled his watchfulness. He had also warned his relief when it was time for that individual to take over.

And he was still suspicious.

He drank the remainder of his pink gin and ordered another. He wasn't particularly fond of pink gin but he could drink more of it than any other drink without ill-effect.

As the white-coated barman set the fresh glass before him, he saw Race and Katrina enter the bar. They spotted him and casually took the vacant place beside him. Race ordered two dry Martinis. Gilmour moved to make room for Katrina. She thanked him and they got into conversation. It was done quite naturally.

"Well?" murmured Race, after a few desultory remarks.

"Seems to be," replied Gilmour. "Nothing much could happen here, anyhow."

"Anything could happen anywhere," said Race. "Yu-Malu has just put in an appearance. She's in the lounge. Keep your eyes skinned."

Gilmour took a sip of pink gin.

"Walker and his bird are going to the Casino tonight," he said. "She's dining with him first."

"Where?"

"Here."

"How do you know?"

"I overheard them talking about it."

"Who's idea was the Casino?"

"Hers. He asked her what she'd like to do."

Race picked up his frosted glass and drank some of his Martini. Still holding the glass he said:

"Don't let Walker out of your sight. We'll keep an eye on Yu-Malu."

"If she tries anything in the Casino she's crazy."

"Don't rely on that. People are never prepared for the unexpected."

He looked across the bar as the lowly companion of the man they were discussing uttered a musical laugh at something he had said. She reached out a slim hand and laid it on his arm in gentle protest.

The light struck a spark of green fire from the ring on her finger.

CHAPTER THREE

The little ivory ball ran round the outer rim of the wheel, hesitated for a split second, and fell into a numbered slot.

"Neuf. Le rouge gagne, impair et manque," the croupier intoned. With an expressionless face he pushed a huge pile of plaques towards Yu-Malu with his rake. Almost disinterestedly she added them to the already large pile in front of her. She had won four times running playing in maximums.

Dressed in an evening gown that set off her extraordinary beauty to perfection and was the envy and admiration of every woman even in that well-dressed throng, Yu-Malu sat next to the *chef de partie* at Roulette Table Number 1 in the big, ornate *salle* of the Casino. Her entrance had caused something of a mild sensation and there was quite a crowd round the table at which she sat. But for all the notice she took of anyone she might have been alone.

"Messieurs, mesdames, fait vous jeux."

In his slightly bored, completely level voice the croupier announced his invitation. Yu-Malu waited until all the other stakes had been placed, and then almost disdainfully, she selected the maximum from her pile of winnings and placed it on the same number as before.

There was a slight whisper among the spectators. It had already come up twice. It was almost impossible that it would come up again.

Anthony Race, who was watching among the crowd with Gilmour, murmured:

"The woman's got the luck of the devil."

"That's more than Walker has," grunted Gilmour. "He hasn't had a win yet."

Walker and his lovely companion were sitting almost opposite the Dragon Princess, and the scientist was looking a little disgruntled.

The croupier picked up the ivory ball, spun the wheel with a slight twist, and almost in the same motion, flicked the ball round the outer rim.

There was dead silence as it rattled round the top of the slots and finally fell into the nine.

"Neuf. Le rouge gagne, impair et manque."

Yu-Malu had won again.

Amid a ripple of excitement from the watching crowd, the croupier pushed the pile of plaques towards her. Calmly she added it to the pile in front of her, rose gracefully to her feet and signalled to a *huissier*. Indicating the pile of plaques, Yu-Malu ordered him to bring them to the *caisse*. Almost disdainfully she threw a plaque of ten mille to the croupier and followed the *huissier*, the crowd parting to let her through.

The girl with Mark Walker passed her hand across

her eyes and murmured something to her companion. From her handbag she took out a pair of dark glasses and put them on.

Anthony Race was watching Yu-Malu so neither he nor Gilmour saw the action. Neither did they see two other very beautiful girls among the crowd follow the example of the girl with Walker and put on dark glasses, as though the lights were hurting their eyes.

With the grace that a professional model would have envied, Yu-Malu made her way to the *caisse*. Here her plaques were exchanged for notes which, after giving the *huissier* a mille francs, she put carelessly in her handbag. Then she, too, took out a pair of dark glasses and carefully adjusted them over her eyes. She also took out of the bag something else—a small object that looked like a cigarette lighter.

By a strange coincidence the girl with Walker had drawn a similar object from her bag and so had the other two girls who looked so exactly alike that they might have been twins.

And then it happened.

The girl with Walker pressed a tiny lever on the little 'lighter'. There was a blinding flash of light—a searing, dazzling glare that was so bright it blinded all those who were not protected from its rays by the special glasses worn by Yu-Malu and her Dragonflies.

At the same instant, Yu-Malu pressed a lever on her 'lighter' and the other two girls did the same to the 'lighters' they held in their dainty fingers.

There was pandemonium. The screams of women

blended with the cursing of men and the shouting of the officials. Race felt as though a black curtain had been suddenly whipped over his head. His eyes burned and ached. Somebody bumped into him but he couldn't see. He was blind. Amid the uproar around him and the shouting and the screaming he tried to grope his way towards Walker. But he was jostled and shoved until he lost all sense of direction.

So this was the meaning of the presence of Yu-Malu. The Dragon Princess had planned this coup with the purpose of getting hold of Mark Walker. This blindness must be the result of one of her damned inventions...

A blind Walker felt his arm gripped gently and the soft voice of his beautiful companion whisper;

"Keep close to me. I'll guide you outside."

"What's happened? I can't see. Everything's dark...."

"I know. It's all right. I'll look after you...."

"But—this is terrible! How can I have suddenly...."

"Don't worry. It won't last—not more than half an hour. Come."

She led him through the panic stricken crowd to the exit where they were joined by Yu-Malu and the two other Dragonflies.

"Look here, I don't understand...," began Walker.

"You don't need to, Mr. Walker," murmured the Dragon Princess. "You only have to do as you are told."

"Who are you? I don't know...."

"I am Yu-Malu. You are coming with me on a little journey."

A fast car was waiting outside the Casino. Still arguing and protesting, Walker was hustled into it, Yu-Malu and the two Dragonflies got in the back. The other Dragonfly slipped behind the wheel. The engine started at a touch and the powerful car shot away just as the van of the frightened crowd in the Casino began to trickle out of the entrance.

****

Katrina Evans had not accompanied her employer, Anthony Race, to the Casino for the simple reason that he had instructed her, much to her annoyance to wait at the hotel and take a call that he was expecting from London. It was not even a very important call, she thought crossly, as she waited impatiently in the lounge. It would have been quite easy to let them ring again.

However, the call came though at last and she listened to a rather dithering official expressing some extremely futile views concerning Walker. When, at last, she had succeeded in cutting short his wholly unoriginal remarks about the weather, she slammed down the receiver and hurried out to her car.

With the result that she reached the Casino just in time to see Yu-Malu and her beautiful assistants hustle Mark Walker into a car.

Katrina never hesitated. She guessed from the noise of screaming and shouting that came from the Casino that something had gone wrong. Somehow the Dragon Princess had managed to get hold of Walker in spite of Race and Gilmour, so, when the car containing Yu-Malu and Walker roared down the coast road, Katrina was not very far behind.

She did not find it very easy. The car belonging to Yu-Malu had a high-powered, super-charged engine, and had she selected to let it all out, Katrina's less powerful car would not have stood a chance. But for some reason, possibly because she did not want any trouble with speed regulations and the chance of being held up by the police, Yu-Malu kept the speed down.

They sped along the winding coast road, Katrina keeping as far away as she dared without risking losing her quarry. At first there was quite a lot of traffic hut this dwindled to nothing as they got farther out into the country.

Katrina wondered where they were going and received an almost immediate answer as the car in front slowed and swung through an open gate into a large field. Katrina pulled up and slipped out of her car, switching off the lights as she did so.

Yu-Malu's car had come to a stop in the middle of the field and as it did so Katrina heard the drone of another engine.

It came from the air.

Katrina crept very cautiously through the gate. The field contained some straggling bushes near the entrance and she took cover among them. The droning engine grew louder. From the car belonging to Yu-Malu a light flashed skywards. It flashed twice and then was dark.

Something came swishing down out of the night sky—a helicopter.

It touched down within a few yards of the car. Yu-Malu had got out of the car and Katrina could dimly make out the figure of Mark Walker between two girls....

"What are you doing here?"

Katrina looked round quickly. A girl was standing watching her! She scrambled to her feet but the girl threw herself on her and knocked her back on the ground.

"I'll teach you to spy on us!" hissed the girl viciously and her hands closed round Katrina's throat.

* * * * * * *

"You may as well come quietly, Mr. Walker," said Yu-Malu in her low, musical voice. "You will come anyway."

"I can't see...what is the matter with my eyes? That light...."

"You will recover very soon. The Celestial Light is only temporary. It numbs the optic nerves but it does not last. However, it is most effective while it does. Now come along."

"I'm not going with you...."

"Very well. You force me to do this...."

Mark Walker felt a sudden sharp prick in his arm, and then he felt nothing.

"Take him to the helicopter," ordered Yu-Malu.

Two other Dragonflies had appeared out of the night.

They had come in the helicopter. They took charge of the senseless man and half dragged half carried him to the waiting machine. Yu-Malu looked round. The two Dragonflies who had been in the Casino were busy fixing something to the car.

"Where's D.7?" asked the Dragon Princess sharply.

"Coming!" called a voice, and the girl ran towards the others, adjusting the thin rubber mask, which they all wore so that they all looked exactly alike. These masks were beautifully made. Fitting skin-tight they were undetectable.

"What have you been doing?" asked Yu-Malu.

"There was someone spying on us. I had to deal with her," the Dragonfly explained a little breathlessly.

"Good! Now, hurry! We do not wish to delay."

Yu-Malu led the way to the helicopter. The rotors were revolving slowly as she climbed aboard and joined her two followers and Walker. The three other Dragonflies came hurrying up, the door was closed and the rotors revved up. The helicopter lifted, soared up into the night sky, and swung out to sea.

"Now!" snapped the Dragon Princess.

The girl at the controls pressed a switch. The radio controlled detonator, which had been fixed to a charge of explosive on the car fired and with a brilliant flash and a shattering roar the car blew up into a thousand pieces.

* * * * * *

Anthony Race and Brian Gilmour heard the sound

of the explosion as they raced along the coast road. The blindness had worn off. Except for headaches they were little the worse. A passerby had seen Yu-Malu's car drive away and recognized the Dragon Princess from Race's description. They had hurried in pursuit but had seen nothing of the car they were in search of.

"What the hell was that?" demanded Gilmour.

"Here, look out! There's a car there without lights. You nearly went into it!"

Race brought the car to a skidding stop.

"That's Katrina's car," he cried as his headlights picked it out.

"Katrina's?"

"She must've followed Yu-Malu," Race jumped out of the car. "Perhaps she's in that field. That's where the explosion came from...."

He hurried through the open gate, followed by Gilmour. A heap of glowing wreckage littered the field—all that remained of Yu-Malu's escape car.

"Katrina!" Race called but there was no reply.

"There's someone over here," called Gilmour. "Over in those bushes."

Race joined him. The body of a girl lay face downwards in the rank grass. Race felt his heart leap. It was Katrina. He recognized the dress she wore, although it was torn and half off.

"Is she still alive?"

Race didn't answer. Very gently he turned the body over. And then he got the shock of his life. The face that looked sightlessly up at him was beautiful and completely strange.

"Who the devil's that?" grunted Gilmour.

"I don't know...."

"She's wearing Katrina's dress."

"Katrina's changed places with one of Yu-Malu's followers. The damned fool! They'll spot her...."

"Well, they've got Walker. There'll be hell to pay over that...."

"Oh, to blazes with Walker!" snapped Race. "That isn't important. It's Katrina I'm worried about...." He rose to his feet. "When Yu-Malu discovers her...."

He broke off. His face was white and strained. He had no illusions concerning the Dragon Princess. She would be quite ruthless.

CHAPTER FOUR

The helicopter did not take them very far. After crossing the coast it swung round in a wide sweep and headed inland.

The Dragonfly at the controls kept a sharp look out, and presently below them appeared a winking light. The helicopter began to drop quickly until it touched down in a large field.

Near where it had come to rest was a sleek-looking plane. Katrina, keeping as much as she could in the background, although the thin rubber mask she had taken from the girl who had attacked her concealed her real appearance, watched them making preparations to transfer Walker to the plane.

He was still unconscious from the drug that had been injected into his veins. Swiftly, but with unhurried precision Yu-Malu directed operations.

In less than fifteen minutes the helicopter had taken off again and they were all inside the waiting plane. This was fitted up in the most luxuriant style and Katrina concluded that it must be a special plane belonging to Yu-Malu. In this she was right. It had flown from the Dragon Princess's, island headquarters to rendezvous at the field in Normandy—timed to a split second. Yu-Malu's planning and organizing were perfect.

The sound of the departing helicopter had scarcely faded away before, at a signal from Yu-Malu, the plane roared across the field and slid easily into the air. It was piloted by another of the Dragon Princess's innumerable girls. Katrina wondered how many she had under her command. However many there were, she thought, grimly, there was one less now.

It had been touch and go in the field at Monte Carlo when her attacker's hands had closed round her throat. She had made no attempt to pull them away, which most people would have done. Instead, she allowed herself to go limp, brought up her right hand and with the edge of it cut the girl on the back of her neck. It was the killer cut! The girl died instantly, falling on her opponent. Katrina had scrambled up, hurriedly changed clothes, and, finding the mask, stripped it off the dead girl and put it on. The idea to take her place had come as a flash of inspiration. If she had given herself time to think she might have hesitated. But there was no time; as it was she barely made it.

The plane was flying high and at speed. Katrina had no idea where they were going, but she wasn't left long in doubt.

"When we reach headquarters," said Yu-Malu, "you, D.7, and you, D.9, will look after this man, Walker. You will stay with him until he recovers from the drug and then you will bring him to me in my private apartments. You understand?"

"Yes, your Highness," one of the girls replied.

Yu-Malu looked at Katrina.

"Did you hear, D.7?"

Katrina realized that she meant her.

"Yes, your Highness."

Obviously these women who assisted Yu-Malu were known by numbers prefixed by the letter 'D'. She was 'D.7'. She would have to remember that.

Yu-Malu was still looking at her curiously. Had she any suspicion that she wasn't the girl she ought to have been! Katrina felt her flesh creep. What would happen to her if the Dragon Princess found out that she was a spy? There was one thing she had forgotten in her hurry—she had forgotten to remove the ring the dead girl had been wearing. She noticed that all the other girls were wearing a similar ring—a large green stone on which was inscribed a dragon. Yu-Malu, herself, wore one. She covered her hand with her other one.

Yu-Malu had turned away. She took her jewelled cigarette case from her handbag, selected one of her tiny cigarettes with its petalled tip, and lit it from a small lighter. Leaning back in the cushioned seat, the Dragon Princess looked out the side window of the plane, smoking thoughtfully.

How long, thought Katrina, would her deception last? Long enough to enable her to take some action? Could she manage to get a message through to Race in some way? Would there be a radio transmitter in these headquarters to which they were going? If so could she get to it?

The plane flew on steadily, high above a layer of cloud that cut off all sight of what was below. Presently it began to lose height. They came through the cloud and Katrina caught a glimpse of the sea. It stretched away on all sides with no sign of land.... Wait. Ahead was a dark patch—a small oasis in the waste of water.

An island. Was this the headquarters they were making for? The plane was coming down in a long gliding sweep, getting lower and lower. Katrina could sec the island more clearly now—a desolate, barren-looking, rocky mass that jutted out of the sea. Low hills covered it with some trees and vegetation but there was no sign of life or habitation....

The plane swept down over a hill and there, invisible until now, was the smooth surface of a runway.

In a few minutes they would land. This, then, was the lair of the Dragon Princess....

* * * * * * *

The man on the bed stirred uneasily, drew in his breath with a deep sighing sound, and opened his eyes. For a moment everything was blurred and out of focus and then, as his sight cleared, he saw that he was in a small room furnished with the bare necessities for a bedroom.

"Mr. Walker."

It was a girl's voice that spoke softly. He struggled up on to one elbow, shaking his head to clear the last remaining mists from his eyes. A girl was bending over him, her eyes anxious and a little fearful.

"Where have I got to? Who are you?"

His voice was husky and scarcely audible.

"Hush!" She put out a hand and touched him lightly. "Don't speak too loud. My name is Katrina—Katrina Evans. I work for Anthony Race...."

"What the devil happened? How did I get here?"

Keeping her voice to little more than a whisper, she told him as briefly as possible.

"Phew!" He passed a hand across his forehead. "We seem to be in the soup...."

"I'm going to try and get a message to Mr. Race," she said in the same low tone. "There must be some form of radio communication, if I can find it...."

"If they find out who you are," he began and stopped as the door slid back and a girl came in. He looked at her in astonishment for she was exactly like Katrina in dress and in looks. He guessed, after the first shock of surprise, that she was wearing one of the thin rubber masks that made all Yu-Malu's followers look alike.

"Her Highness wishes to see you at once," said the girl. "You will follow me. You will accompany us D.7."

"I hope her Highness has got a good explanation for bringing me here," he said, swinging his legs off the bed and getting gingerly to his feet.

"Her Highness will explain just as much as she wishes to explain," answered the Dragonfly. "Come."

She took him by the arm and led him to the door. Katrina followed. Outside was a wide corridor. It was brilliantly lit and the walls consisted of glass behind which tropical fish swam lazily among rocks and weedy grottoes, their brilliant colours flashing in the light. The corridor branched into another, and behind the glass walls of this were strange and hideous reptiles and insects. A large, bloated spider looked at them with venomous, beady eyes as they hurried past. Farther along were queer, unhealthy-looking fungi and tropical plants. It was a weird setting but they had no time to see it properly.

They came, at last, to a wide archway beyond which was a blank wall. The girl with them took a silver whistle from her bag. Putting it to her lips she blew gently. There was no sound but the wall rose like a portcullis. Beyond was a polished door.

"Come in," said the voice of Yu-Malu softly.

The door swung open and they entered a wide, exquisitely furnished hall. Their guide put away her whistle and led the way over to another door that faced the entrance. This, too, opened at their approach and they found themselves in a large and lovely room. On every side were priceless pieces of antique furniture, beautiful examples of ivory carving, and Chinese porcelain. The hangings were silken tapestries, beautifully worked in threads of gold and silver and glowing colours.

In a cushioned chair beside an inlaid table on which stood a tea set of fabulous Ming china, sat Yu-Malu. She had changed into a robe of heavy, cream coloured silk on which emerald hued dragons writhed and twisted— a marvellous example of Chinese embroidery.

"Welcome, Mr. Walker," said Yu-Malu. "Please sit down. I trust you are quite recovered?"

"I should like to know why I have been brought here?" he said curtly.

Yu-Malu laughed, her musical ripple of merriment that was like the chiming of silver bells.

"You are very direct, Mr. Walker. We shall come to that in good time. You would like some tea?"

"No, thank you."

"Come, Mr. Walker! Aren't you being a little ungracious? I am prepared to treat you as an honoured guest...."

"You have dragged me here by force...."

"Had I thought you would have accepted an invitation I would have issued one. You had better sit down. We have a lot to discuss."

Yu-Malu made a sign to Katrina and the other girl. The Dragonfly turned to the door and Katrina thought she had better follow her. She would have liked to stay and hear what happened.

When they had gone and the door was dosed, the Dragon Princess leaned back in her chair and crossed her legs. The robe slid away from her knees exhibiting her beautifully shaped legs.

"Sit down," she said again. "There are cigarettes on the table beside the chair."

He sat down. The overpowering personality of the woman was difficult to withstand. The air was full of a strange and subtle perfume—the perfume that was specially distilled and blended for Yu-Malu in her own laboratories.

"I will be quite frank with you, Mr. Walker," said Yu-Malu. "I have need of your rocket fuel formula for China...."

"Is that why you went to all this trouble?" he interrupted her.

"That is why...."

"Then you've had all your trouble for nothing."

"I think not." She reached over and took one of her tiny, petal-tipped cigarettes from an ivory box on the table. "I should advise you to cooperate with me. If you do I can promise you a very pleasant and comfortable stay here. My laboratories are of the latest design and contain the most modern equipment in the world—a great deal of equipment that the world has, as yet, no knowledge of. These are at your disposal...."

"Supposing I don't cooperate?"

Yu-Malu very carefully lit her cigarette. She put down the jewelled lighter. She blew out a thin cloud of smoke from between her beautifully moulded lips.

She said, in a level voice:

"I have many methods at my disposal to—persuade you, Mr. Walker."

He laughed.

"Nothing you could do would persuade me to give you the formula," he said.

"We shall see." She looked at him quite calmly. "I have dealt with many difficult people, Mr. Walker. After treatment they have no longer been difficult...."

"But this is different," he said.

She raised her eyebrows slightly.

"Different?"

"You've made a mistake," he said. "I couldn't give you the formula because I don't know what it is."

Yu-Malu frowned.

"Come, Mr. Walker, you are being foolish...."

"It's you who are foolish," he broke in. "You see: I'm not Mark Walker. You've got hold of the wrong man."

CHAPTER FIVE

For a second the beautiful face of the Dragon Princess changed. All the accumulated evil that lay behind that lovely exterior flashed for a moment in the suddenly distorted features. The man before her wondered why he had ever thought her beautiful....

And then, once more, she was the same as before. Only her eyes were hard, like splinters of ice.

"It will do you no good to lie," she said.

"I'm telling the truth!" he asserted. "I'm not Mark Walker. I'm not even a scientist. I don't know a test tube from an egg-boiler!"

"I do not believe you. This is a trick to deceive me. But it will not avail you." She reached out her hand and touched a concealed switch in the table beside her chair. "Sin Wu, I require you in my apartment at once. Bring the drug of truth."

"I come immediately, your Highness." The voice of the old Chinaman came from somewhere in the room.

Yu-Malu leaned back. She had regained control of herself. Through half-closed eyes she surveyed the man in the chair before her.

"No doubt," she said, "you expect that I shall accept

what you say...."

"Whether you accept it or not makes no difference," he retorted. "What I've told you is the truth. I couldn't give you a formula for cough mixture...."

"We shall see. If you are speaking the truth I shall soon know. It will be better for you if you are lying. That way there would be a chance for you."

She didn't raise her voice. It was still low and musical, but there was a menace in it that sent a chill down his spine.

This woman would be quite ruthless if she were thwarted. She would kill with as little emotion as she would light her cigarette.

The door opened and Sin Wu came softly into the room. He carried in his hand a small inlaid box.

"This man asserts that he is not Mark Walker," said Yu-Malu. "I wish to learn the truth."

"The truth shall be yours, your Highness," said the old man. He put down the box on a nearby table and slid back the lid. From the interior he took out a small hypodermic syringe and a crystal phial that was half full of a colourless liquid. Removing the stopper, he plunged the needle of the syringe into the little bottle and drew up a small quantity of the liquid.

"This will not hurt you," he said as he approached the pseudo Walker. "It is a preparation of our own discovery which acts on the mind in such a way that it is impossible to lie...."

"You keep away."

"Do not be foolish."

Sin Wu with surprising strength gripped him by the shoulder and stopped him getting up. The needle of the syringe was thrust into his arm and the plunger pressed home. The sharp prick was all he felt. There was no other sensation at all. And then all initiative seemed to evaporate from him. He couldn't think....

"Who are you?" He heard the voice of Yu-Malu as from a great distance.

"Peter Dale," he answered promptly.

"Why did you pretend to be Mark Walker?"

"I was ordered to do so."

"Who by?"

"British counter-espionage."

"Why?"

"I don't know."

"Where is Mark Walker?"

"I don't know."

The low, monotonous voice of Yu-Malu went on and on, repeating questions she had asked before and adding others until she had discovered everything about Peter Dale that she wanted to know. At last, wearily, she stopped.

"There is no doubt," she said to Sin Wu who had stood motionless during her examination. "I made an error. He shall pay for it—all those concerned shall pay. Take him away, Sin Wu. I will see him again when the effect of the truth drug has worn off. I wish him to be in full possession of his mental powers when I pass sentence upon him."

* * * * * * *

Brian Gilmour and Anthony Race sat in the latter's bedroom in the Hotel Splendide. They both looked worn and worried.

"Why didn't you tell me that you'd substituted this man, Dale, for Mark Walker?" asked Gilmour after a long silence.

"Because the fewer people who knew the better," said Race. "Even Katrina didn't know. It was my idea. I was hoping that Yu-Malu would rise to the bait...."

"She did."

"Yes. But it didn't quite work out as I intended. However, there's still a chance that it will. She must have taken them both back to wherever she has her headquarters...."

"And you hope that they'll be able to get a message back?"

"There's a chance. Peter Dale isn't a fool and Katrina's got her head screwed on the right way. If there's any way of getting a message back, they'll do it."

"And if they don't?"

Race frowned.

"I'm not allowing myself to think of that," he said.

"Where is the real Walker?"

"Spending a very quiet holiday in a little village in Cornwall." He rose to his feet. "Come down to the bar and have a drink."

"And after that?"

"We might as well go back to London. There's no point in remaining here."

* * * * * * *

Peter Dale stood before the Dragon Princess. The effects of the drug had worn off and he was in full control of his wits. He wondered what she was going to do with him.

She had changed into a plain but beautifully cut dress that clung tightly to her lovely figure. She looked, he thought, every inch a princess. It was a pity that he had caught a glimpse of the real woman during that moment of consummate rage when the mask had slipped....

"I now know all about you, Mr. Dale," she said evenly. "What you told me in the first place was the truth. It only remains for me to decide what your punishment is to be."

"And that you have already decided," he said.

She inclined her head.

"I have, as you are aware, a number of very beautiful girls who are dedicated to the same aims as I am myself. They come from all countries. They are known as the Dragonflies. They do not have much amusement, Mr. Dale. We have few presentable young men in these headquarters of mine and it is only natural that my Dragonflies should miss the society and—er—other amenities that a young and healthy man could supply. You understand my meaning?"

He nodded. There was no mistaking what she meant. But there must be more to it than that...

"A starving dog welcomes the bone that is flung to it," continued Yu-Malu. "A pack of starving dogs will behave in a similar manner. I propose to make you the bone, Mr. Dale. I shall give you to my Dragonflies."

She paused and smiled. It was not a nice smile.

"You don't think that is a very terrible punishment, Mr. Dale?"

"It doesn't sound like a punishment at all," he began and she stopped him with a gesture of one of her lovely hands.

"Wait, Mr. Dale," she said. "There is more to come. When my Dragonflies have been satisfied, you will be taken to one of my operating theatres. We have surgeons here. A man in the full strength of his manhood cannot be allowed to remain among a number of attractive women. The domestic cat, if he is a male, suffers in the same way. I have often thought it cruel to rob him of his pleasures."

He stared at the smiling face of this woman who looked so lovely. She couldn't possibly mean...?

"Oh, yes, Mr. Dale," she said, answering his unspoken question. "I mean exactly that."

Katrina had been left to her own devices after she had been dismissed by Yu-Malu after conducting Dale to the Dragon Princess's apartments. Nobody seemed to bother about her. Obviously, as yet, she remained unsuspected. The thing to do was to take advantage of this respite that might be shorter than she hoped.

She had seen nothing more of Peter Dale. She had peeped into the bedroom where he had been first taken to but it was empty.

She decided to explore this underground hideout of Yu-Malu's. Surely there must be some kind of radio communication with the mainland. It was unlikely that the Dragon Princess would be willing to stay here completely cut off. If there were such an installation Katrina was determined to find it.

It was a vast place. There were numerous bedrooms in the living quarters, a large restaurant from which the kitchens opened. All these various departments were linked by numberless corridors, white painted and lit by concealed lighting, the walls in most cases consisting of glass-fronted tanks in which multi-hued fish swam lazily. There were other less pleasant things—ugly looking insects and reptiles and rather sinister orchids and fungi.

Katrina during her exploration saw several people, men of the Chinese coolie type and a number of the Dragonflies, but they took no notice of her. They were all going about their own business and seemed to accept her as one of themselves.

From what she could make out, the layout of the place was roughly like a wheel, with Yu-Malu's private apartments forming the hub. The huge cave with the enormous lift that she had seen on her first arrival was entirely separate to the rest of the place connected to the main part by a wide, plain corridor.

But she found nothing in the way of a radio installation. But there must be something of the sort she thought. Doggedly and rather desperately, she continued her search. Up one corridor and down another she went. They all looked alike that was the difficulty. And then, quite by accident she found what she was seeking.

She had paused at the junction of two corridors trying to make up her mind which way to go when she saw part of the floor slide back and the head and shoulders of a girl appeared. She was not wearing one of the thin rubber masks and she was dressed in spotless white overalls. Katrina stepped back, concealing herself in the angle of the wall. The girl came up into the corridor, went over to a buttress that supported the roof and pressed her finger against something. The floor slid back into place.

The girl hurried away along the corridor. Katrina waited until she was gone and then she went over and examined the buttress. Almost invisible, set in the stone were two small buttons. She pressed one of them but nothing happened. She pressed the other and immediately the floor slid back. The first button must control the shutting mechanism, she thought.

With her heart beating faster, she went over to the oblong trap in the floor. A flight of stone steps led downwards. She looked quickly round. The corridor was deserted. Stealthily she began to descend the steps. They were quite short and she found herself in another corridor at a lower level. Before her was a door with 'Danger' painted on it in red lettering. She went over to it and just as she reached it, it slid. A man confronted her—a Chinaman in a grey uniform with a green dragon across the breast.

"What do you do here?" he demanded. "You know that this is out of bounds to all except the Princess and the technicians. Who are you?"

Katrina could see beyond him that she had found what she had been seeking. The room was filled with radio equipment.

"Her Highness sent me with a message," she replied, saying the first thing she could think of. And it was the wrong thing.

"Her Highness would have come through on the intercom system," he retorted. "You have no right here. Who are you?"

Katrina held out her hand, half-closed as though she had something in it. He bent forward to peer into the palm and she swung her other hand up in a sharp cut to his neck.

But it did not reach the right spot. He ducked and the edge of her hand caught him on the side of his neck instead of the back. It was sufficient, however, to send him staggering. Before he had time to recover his balance she made a dart for the steps. She was up them like a flash but as she climbed through the trap she heard the shrill clangour of bells from near and far.

The alarm had been given.

CHAPTER SIX

In Yu-Malu's private apartment a buzzer sounded sharply. On the wall facing the chair in which she sat a red light glowed. With an exclamation the Dragon Princess touched a switch on the table be-side her. A picture slid back revealing a television screen on which was a scene depicting Katrina near the open trap in the floor of the corridor. At the same time a man's voice began to gabble quickly in Chinese.

Peter Dale, recovering from the shock that she had given him when she told him what was going to happen to him, couldn't understand what was said, but he gathered from what he saw that Katrina had been caught.

Yu-Malu was replying in a flood of Chinese. He gathered that there must be a concealed microphone in the table because she was leaning forward as she spoke.

The picture on the screen showed Katrina fleeing along the corridor. As she turned the corner into another corridor, the hidden television camera picked her up on the closed circuit and transmitted the picture to Yu-Malu's receiver.

The Dragon Princess touched another switch.

"Close all bulkheads in section 'R'," she ordered in English. She turned to Dale. "You shall see how we deal with people who do not obey orders. One of my Dragonflies has been so indiscreet as to venture near the radio room...."

So she didn't know who Katrina was, thought Dale.

"Watch!" murmured Yu-Malu.

On the screen he saw Katrina running as fast as she could along a corridor. And suddenly in front of her a door slid down blocking her path. She had only just tune to pull up and prevent herself running into it. She turned and sped in the opposite direction, but another door slid down again blocking her way.

Yu-Malu laughed, her silvery distinctive laugh.

Katrina turned into a side corridor. She was allowed to reach nearly the end of it before the barrier came down. As she retraced her steps the entrance to the corridor was blocked by another sliding barrier. Katrina stopped, panting heavily. She looked from left to right like a trapped animal. There was fear in her eyes, and Yu-Malu's laughter increased.

"It is a pity we cannot continue the game," she said. "Bring the woman to me!"

Katrina was still searching for some way out of her prison when the door at one end of the corridor slid up. She turned towards it hopefully, but the way beyond was blocked with Dragonflies!

They were all unmasked and looked to Dale like a bevy of beauty queens—only the expressions on their lovely faces were unpleasantly vicious. They surrounded Katrina, pulling her this way and that.

"Bring her to me!" ordered Yu-Malu and pressed a switch. The picture faded from the screen and the painting slid back into place.

"She shall suffer for her disobedience," said the Dragon Princess. She took one of her tiny cigarettes and lit it. "You shall see, Mr. Dale, how we punish disobedience."

"What has she done?" he asked.

"She has violated one of the strict rules of my establishment. She has been inquisitive. No one—I repeat—no one is allowed near the radio installation except myself and my technicians. Those orders are inviolate. All my Dragonflies are taught to obey me without question. For some reason, which I shall find out, this one has elected to disobey. She will regret it."

Dale remained silent. There was nothing he could do. Katrina had bravely made her attempt and failed. She probably wouldn't get another chance

A swarm of Dragonflies brought her in. Her hair had fallen about her shoulders and her dress was half torn off. She still, however, wore the thin rubber mask.

"Stand away from her!" said Yu-Malu. "Now—take off that mask!"

Katrina stood in front of her defiantly.

"Take it off!"

Reluctantly Katrina obeyed.

"Who are you? You are not D.7." Yu-Malu rose to her feet and approached the girl. Dale had never realized before that Katrina was beautiful. The severe way she was accustomed to wearing her hair and the style in which she dressed had concealed the fact she was as lovely as any of the girls who were with her.

"Who are you? Where is the real D.7?"

Katrina remained silent.

"You must be in league with this man," said Yu-Malu. "He has confessed that he is a British agent and not Mark Walker."

Katrina's face expressed her astonishment. She had not been in Race's confidence. She had not known that he was anything but the real Walker.

"You are a good actress," said Yu-Malu.

"She didn't know," broke in Dale.

"Then why is she here?"

Dale shrugged his shoulders.

"I've no idea...."

"Somehow you changed places with the real D.7," said Yu-Malu. "Very well. I will give you a choice. You can swear allegiance to me and remain here as one of my Dragonflies or you can undergo The Ecstasy of the Seventh Beatitude...."

There was a sudden hissing of sharply indrawn breath from the girls behind her. It was a gasp of horror. Obviously, they knew what the Dragon Princess referred to.

"Choose!"

Katrina looked at her. There was contempt in her eyes but she said nothing.

"Strip her!" ordered Yu-Malu.

The Dragonflies swarmed round Katrina. They

tore her clothes from her, leaving her as naked as the day she was born. Katrina flinched but she remained defiant.

Yu-Malu uttered her distinctive laugh.

"You would have made an excellent Dragonfly," she said, surveying the rounded curves of the lovely body before her. "Take her to The Place of Beatitude." She turned to Dale. "You shall witness this with me. It will be both interesting and instructive."

"What is The Seventh Beatitude?" he asked hoarsely.

CHAPTER SEVEN

"If you require anything," said the Dragonfly, a lovely brunette who had been delegated to take Dale back to his bedroom, "press that button." She indicated an ivory button set in the polished wood of the bedhead. "One of us will answer you at once. But don't try and escape or attempt to leave this room. It is well guarded and you will be killed."

She smiled, looking him over as though he were some prize animal.

"You're the best man I've seen for a long time," she sighed, "Oh, such a long time. I hope I'm the lucky one!"

He raised his eyebrows.

"The lucky one?"

"The first to get you," she explained calmly. "We are going to draw lots, you see—with cards—"

"Was that awful woman serious?" he began, and stopped as the Dragonfly raised her arm and brought her open hand with a resounding smack across his face!

"You will always refer to the Princess Yu-Malu as 'Her Highness'," she said. "Remember that!"

"You vicious little cat!" He caught her wrist, but her

other hand was pressing a curiously shaped gun into his stomach.

"I should hate to spoil our fun by injuring you," she said. "This gun would blow your guts out if I press the trigger."

Peter Dale dabbed at his cheek. Her ring had cut him and drawn blood.

"Charming lot, aren't you?" he grunted.

"I'll make it up to you—if I'm lucky enough to win the first draw," she said.

"How many draws are there?"

"Until we've all been allotted our turn...."

"I hope you allow a decent interval between turns," said Peter with a grimace.

She laughed. She had lovely teeth, very even and very white.

"Don't worry! We don't want anyone to be disappointed...."

"Does your recent addition join the ranks?" he asked, thinking of Katrina.

She shook her head.

"Certainly not! She is a conscript. She will not be allowed any privileges." She turned to the exit. "I hope to see you soon," she said and went out.

Dale flung himself on the bed. So there wasn't going to be any chance of a word with Katrina, he thought. He wondered what had happened to her after she had been taken from the torture room. Probably she was recovering from her ordeal. It must have been pretty nerve racking. He still felt sick at the memory of it....

This was the most amazing set-up he had ever come up against. Yu-Malu was a fiend. The punishment she had selected for him was scarcely the action of a sane woman. But she was sane. Not only sane but brilliantly clever, a kind of perverted genius! A woman obsessed with one idea—China. And the Dragonflies, those exquisitely lovely girls she had collected around her, they were just as bad. None of them would show the tiniest spark of mercy. They, like the woman they served, were dedicated.

He lay back on the pillow, clasped his hands behind his head, and stared up at the white ceiling. The prospect was not a very cheerful one. After the feast would come the reckoning—and what a reckoning.

He shuddered as he thought of it....

* * * * * * *

Yu-Malu lay on a soft couch. She had just come out of her luxuriously appointed bathroom and she was completely naked. Her maid, armed with delicately perfumed essence, unknown to the Western world, was giving her a massage. The white, smooth skin acquired a rose-petal hue beneath her touch. The firm flesh of the perfect body was without a blemish—the flesh of a young girl in the first flush of her beauty. There was every reason why Yu-Malu had been called the "Most Beautiful Woman in the World."

And yet by natural standards she was old.

Only the secret process, discovered by one of the ancient Llamas of Tibet, kept age at bay....

The Chinese maid finished the massage and helped her mistress to rise from the couch. She inducted her into a soft, silken robe, and brought slippers for Yu-MaIu's dainty, well-shaped feet.

The Dragon Princess went over to an ornate cushioned chair and sat down.

"You may send in the hairdresser and bring tea, Tsi Chen," she said.

"Yes, your Highness."

The maid picked up the silver tray with the crystal bottles and jars containing the essences she had used and carried it out.

Yu-Malu helped herself to one of her tiny petal-tipped cigarettes and lit it. In a few minutes an attractive Dragonfly with beautiful auburn hair glided into the apartment, She carried a case of crocodile skin, which she set down on a low table near Yu-Malu.

"How would you like your hair done, your Highness?" she asked. She had once been the leading assistant in a famous New York salon before, through the American branch of the Triad, she had been picked for service with the Dragon Princess.

"Style Number Eight," said Yu-Malu. "Tell me, have the lots yet been drawn for the man, Dale?"

The girl shook her head.

"Not yet, your Highness."

"That is as well. I am leaving in a few hours for England. I shall need to take a team of Dragonflies with me. Those who go with me will be excluded from the draw."

"The pleasure of serving with your Highness will be sufficient compensation," murmured the girl. Deftly she uncoiled Yu-Malu's long and luxuriant hair and it fell about her shoulders. With a gold-backed brush, encrusted with jewels, she began to brush the soft, shining tresses.

The maid entered with the tea. She set down the tray with the saucerless bowl of Ming, poured out tea, milk-less and sugarless, but with a lump of butter, Chinese fashion, and brought it over to her mistress.

"Find Sin Wu," ordered the Dragon Princess. "Tell him I wish to see him."

"Yes, your Highness."

The maid bowed her head and went out.

Yu-Malu sipped her tea. Presently the ancient Chinaman came in softly.

"You may sit, Sin Wu," said Yu-Malu as he stood obsequiously before her.

He bowed and sat on a carven stool facing her.

"I am about to strike my first major blow against the West," said Yu-Malu. "You will see that my plane is prepared and ready to leave in three hours. You will also arrange that my Dragonflies will be in the conference room in one hour."

"It shall be as you desire, your Highness."

"The Gold Disintegrator is to be put on board the plane."

Sin Wu bowed.

"It shall be done, your Highness."

"That is all."

The old man rose slowly to his feet.

"I shall await you in the cavern, your Highness," he said, bowed again, and walked majestically to the door....

* * * * * *

In the big conference room, where the representatives of the Triad met on special occasions, the Dragonflies were lined up on one side of the long table. Yu-Malu, looking more lovely than ever in a plain but beautifully cut suit that looked as if she had been poured into it, faced them from the other side.

"I have told you, briefly, the object of this journey," she was saying. "You will realize that it could be extremely dangerous. I need eight of you to accompany me. In view of the danger, which could result in the death of some of those with me, I shall ask for volunteers. The only two who must be with me are the scientists who understand the working of the Gold Disintegrator. Please raise your right hands, those who wish to accompany me."

The right hand of every girl in the room was raised.

"I might have expected that," said the Dragon Princess. "Very well, I will make my choice. D.1, and D.3, D.5, D.6 and D.10, D.14 and D.15. That leaves one more. You—D.9."

There were murmurs of disappointment from the girls who had not been chosen. The eight who had were told to be at the plane in an hour.

"You will not need much luggage," said Yu-Malu.

"Anything you need can be bought in London...."

She dismissed them.

The plane was waiting when an hour later Yu-Malu arrived in the cavern. The Gold Disintegrator had been placed on board and the two scientists, a specially lovely brunette and an equally beautiful red-head, had already taken their places. The eight Dragonflies who were going with the Dragon Princess clustered round the foot of the steps that led up to the entrance in the fuselage.

Sin Wu came forward as Yu-Malu prepared to board the plane.

"My humble prayers go with you, your Highness. I would wish that you were safely back, your task accomplished."

"I thank you, Sín Wu," said Yu-Malu. "I shall not fail. This will be the first step towards the glories of a reborn China!"

Her eyes flashed and her whole lovely face was transfigured by the fanatical fires that burned within her. She mounted the steps of the plane, and the Dragonflies followed her. The steps were removed and the giant lift on which the plane rested began to ascend slowly.

Sin Wu watched it until it had vanished from sight to the runway above....

* * * * * * *

Peter Dale lay back against the pillows on his bed and smoked a cigarette. He was clad in silk pyjamas, comfortable after a hot shower in the bathroom that was attached to his bedroom.

An excellent meal, complete with a bottle of wine, coffee and brandy had been brought to him, and he had dined well. A box of cigarettes, the suit of pyjamas, dressing gown and slippers, had followed. They had been brought by a dwarf, an ugly-looking fellow with a huge, misshapen head, who mouthed queer uncouth noises at him.

He was a mute.

Whatever horrors lay in store for him, thought Peter, he couldn't complain at his present treatment. The food had been good and well-cooked, the wine a vintage claret. He had thoroughly enjoyed his meal, although he had no illusion concerning his ultimate fate. Yu-Malu had meant what she said and her sentence would be carried out to the letter.

But while there was life there was hope.

Some opportunity might yet occur to escape. In the meanwhile, he may as well make the best of it.

So far as escape was possible, the bedroom, although comfortable, even luxurious, was as tightly sealed as a prison cell. Like all the other rooms in this strange underground headquarters of Yu-Malu there were no windows. Ventilation was catered for by grills high up near the ceiling. The door was tightly fastened and he guessed would be well guarded.

He wondered what had happened to Katrina. If only he could have got a word with her. She would have been able to tell him where the radio room was—just in case...

He raised himself on one elbow, listening. A sound had percolated the silence of the room, a sound like the passing of a train. It came from somewhere below, a faint rumble that set everything in the room vibrating.

Surely there wasn't some kind of underground railway? The sound died away, and once again there was silence. Perhaps there was a railway for carrying stores....

Peter yawned. A glance at his wristwatch told him that it was nearly half past seven. A spot of sleep would do him good, sooth his tensed nerves. He had reached out his hand to turn off the light beside his bed when the door slid back.

A girl stepped quickly into the room and closed the door behind her. She was an ash-blonde. Her hair, so pale a gold that it looked almost silver, fell straightly to her shoulders, curling softly inwards. She wore a robe of black lace, caught in at the waist with a wide ribbon of mauve silk. On her small feet, which peeped from below the billows of lace were heelless mules of the same hue.

She stood looking at him, her red lips slightly parted, her large, deep blue eyes shaded by long lashes, almost expressionless.

"Hello," said Peter. He tried to speak coolly but his pulses were racing as a surge of desire sent the hot blood pumping through his veins.

She smiled; it was a slow, lascivious smile. Very deliberately she untied the silken bow at her waist and let the black lace robe drop to the floor....

* * * * * *

Anthony Race was asleep when the telephone ringing beside his bed awoke him.

Still hazy with sleep, he lifted the receiver. The agitated voice of the high official came crackling over the wire.

"I must see you at once. A most urgent matter. I can't explain on the telephone...."

Race glanced at the dock beside the telephone. It was a quarter to seven.

"Where are you?" he said.

"At the office. I had to come straight away. If there's any truth in this it's a most serious matter...."

"Yu-Malu?"

"Yes, yes." The high official was almost incoherent. "You must come at once...."

"I'll be there in twenty minutes," said Race and rang off.

He took a hasty bath, shaved, dressed and was in Whitehall five minutes later than he had stipulated.

"Now, what's all the trouble?" he demanded, bursting into the high official's office.

"I can't believe that it's possible," said that harassed individual, looking even more incapable than usual.

"If it's Yu-Malu, anything is possible!" retorted Race. "What's it all about? They can't have got you here at this hour for nothing...."

"Everybody's been alerted," said the high official gloomily. "Got me out of bed at six. There was no signature to the message—just a Green Dragon...."

"What message? Look here, suppose you start at the beginning."

"Yes, yes, of course. The beginning." The high official brushed his hand across his eyes as though he were removing a cobweb. "Well, it was one of the grooms at Buckingham Palace who found it. Stuck in the collar of one of Her Majesty's corgis.... Good heavens! The infernal cheek of that bloody woman! Here—read this." He picked a sheet of paper from his desk and held it out. "It's a copy, of course. The Special Branch have got the original...."

Race took the paper. It was headed:

TO ALL WHOM THIS MAY CONCERN
Take Notice

It is our intention to strike a blow at our enemies of the Western world by destroying their existing stock of gold reserve. Britain will be the first to suffer. THIS IS NO IDLE THREAT! To prove that it can be done a demonstration will be carried out at the Salerooms of Sotheby & Company, the famous Auctioneers, in Bond Street. In three days time the internationally famous collection of emeralds known as the Crown of the Incas is to be auctioned. The emeralds are mounted in solid gold. The gold will be destroyed. REMEMBER THIS IS ONLY A DEMONSTRATION. If our demands are complied with there will be no further demonstration. Otherwise...?

The message ended abruptly and significantly. Below was the crude drawing of a green dragon.

"The original Green Dragon was stamped with a rubber stamp," explained the high official. "It must be a hoax. Destroy gold? It's impossible!"

"What are these demands?" asked Race.

"I don't know!" The high official waved his hand irritably. "That's all we've received. Stuck in the collar of one of Her Majesty's corgis! Can you beat it?"

"If the gold reserves were destroyed it would be pretty serious," muttered Race, frowning at the message. "Serious? My dear chap, it would be disastrous."

"Now we know why Yu-Malu was collecting that gold."

The high official's prominent eyes nearly popped out altogether.

"Good Heavens! You mean...? She'd have all the gold in the world...."

"China would—which amounts to the same thing."

The high official looked aghast.

"It's impossible!" he declared feebly. "It can't be done. This blasted woman must be bluffing...."

"I wouldn't rely on that, if I were you," retorted Race grimly.

"Something must be done, it *must* be done. She must be stopped. We can't have a foreign woman threatening us...."

"What," inquired Race gently, "do you suggest that we do?"

The high official gaped at him. Like the majority of

high officials, he had no ideas.

CHAPTER EIGHT

Somehow or other the Press got hold of the story. Before it could be stopped it was blazoned forth to the world at large beneath banner headlines. And the result was near chaos.

Computers and telecommunications became jammed with messages from every corner of the world to the leading banks and exchanges. The whole economic structure of the world was threatened, if the threat contained in the message were carried out.

Peking denied all knowledge of it. Russia was as concerned as were all the other countries.

The wholesale destruction of gold.

It was something unprecedented—something so enormous that the minds of all those who dealt with finance boggled at the possibility. Money could become useless. Just as the mark had become useless after the second World war. Waste paper. Of no value without the gold to back it up.

All over the world the leading bankers held hasty conferences, governments called special cabinet meetings, shares fell heavily on Wall Street and the London Stock Exchange.

The Home Secretary discussed the matter with the heads of Scotland Yard, the Foreign Secretary discussed the matter with the heads of British Intelligence. Nobody came to any satisfactory conclusion.

The Prime Minister, for once lacking any platitudes that would fit the occasion, called a meeting of his cabinet in Downing Street. The Leader of the Opposition, unable to think of any way of coping with the situation, called a meeting of the Shadow Cabinet. Both these gentlemen made speeches full of rhetoric, and meaning precisely nothing.

The Chancellor of the Exchequer pooh-poohed the whole thing.

"How can these people—this woman—whoever is at the bottom of this threat, how do you imagine that they can carry it out?" he said, surveying his colleagues on either side of the long table with a sceptical smile. "It's ridiculous!"

"This demonstration...," began the Foreign Secretary.

"Will fizzle out!" interrupted the Chancellor. "It's a lot of rubbish, in my opinion. Destroy gold? What do they intend to do? Blow it up?"

"I'm inclined to agree with you," said the Prime Minister, "but we must be prepared for all eventualities. We must show strength and determination. We must not let ourselves be coerced into anything that...."

"You don't have to talk all that stuff to us!" broke in the Chancellor rudely. "That's all very well at a public meeting! My opinion is that we are just wasting our time discussing the thing at all. I've got an appointment for lunch and.... Good God!"

"What's the matter?" asked the Home Secretary.

"My watch—look at my watch!" shouted the Chancellor.

"And mine!"

"Look at *my* watch!"

All those present who possessed a gold watch stared incredulously. Nothing remained of the gold except a little heap of grey ash.

At that precise moment an ambulance was passing along Downing Street. In it, dressed in the uniform of a hospital nurse, sat Yu-Malu. She was laughing.

* * * * * *

Peter Dale drained the remainder of a cut glass goblet of brandy and lit a cigarette. The dinner he had just eaten was, as usual, perfect; the wine that had accompanied it could not have been bettered in the best restaurant in the world. But for the shadow that loomed over him and was drawing nearer with each passing hour, he could have been fairly content. He tried to put his ultimate fate out of his mind but it kept on intruding.

This was the morning of the third day since he had been a prisoner. And he had seen no one except the dwarf and his nightly visitor. There had up to now been two, tonight there would be a third. Each one had been physically lovely, eager and avid for the pleasure he could give her. But it was a sheer animal sensuality. There was no tenderness, no trace of softness in their passion-clouded eyes. It was love making without love—without even a pretence of love.

But he had learned something. He had learned the location of the radio room. Either the girl last night had been off her guard or, what was more likely, she didn't think he would be able to make use of the information, and she had told him.

In the back of his mind he had a hazy idea for escape. It might work. In any case it might enable him to get to the radio room. He could take it from there if he were successful. But he wanted one more item of information first. He hoped that he might be able to get it from the girl who was due that night....

* * * * * * *

The British Delegate, Sir Basil Samuels, leaned back in his chair at the National Assembly of the United Nations in New York and waited for the applause that had greeted the speech of the Indian Delegate to die down. It was his turn next. He held the sheaf of notes for his address on International Foreign Policy loosely in his fattish hand. They were fairly detailed. Sir Basil was not a good speaker. He was apt to lose himself unless he followed rigidly the speech that had been prepared for him. Sometimes he wasn't quite sure what he was saying but he always managed to make it sound convincing.

As his name was announced, he rose and took his place before the array of microphones, putting his speech on the table in front of him. During the applause that broke out, he adjusted his spectacles, glanced down at the first page of his speech, and began in his rather sonorous voice....

He gave an outline of British Foreign Policy, full of goodwill and peace on earth to all nations, deplored the troubled state of the world and the need for tolerance between the East and the West. He assured all nations that Britain stood for peace, had always stood for peace, painted a lurid picture of the menace of nuclear war, and how the entire world would become a better and more prosperous place to live in if that menace could be removed, touched lightly on the current conflicts in the East, and came, at last, to the winding up of his peroration.

"The British Government would like to put the following demands to the Assembly. All nuclear weapons belonging to the Western world shall be destroyed. The formula for the new cold rocket fuel shall be made available to China...."

So far he got amid a stunned silence before he realized what he was saying. And then, as his voice trailed away in confusion, and he stared helplessly at the page of notes from which he had been reading, pandemonium broke out.

Delegates shouted abuse, leaping up and waving their arms. Voices screamed in all languages. Everyone tried to shout the others down. In vain, the Secretary-General tried to quell the uproar, but his voice was drowned in the noise. The press cameras flashed like so many exploding bombs, and the reporters from the national press tried to force their way through the gesticulating, yelling crowd to the exists and the nearest telephones.

Sir Basil collapsed in his seat, his face streaming with perspiration at the realization of what he had done.

"Somebody must have substituted that for my original speech," he kept muttering feebly. "I didn't know until I'd read it...."

Somebody *had*.

Yu-Malu's demands had gone out to the world.

* * * * * * *

"That bloody fool, Samuels!" grated the high official almost choking in his rage. "Blundering, blasted, idiot!"

"It's no good going on like that," said Race calmly. "It's done now...."

"Couldn't the incompetent lunatic understand what he was reading?" demanded the high official. "Surely he must have known that...."

"The only thing that matters now is that we know Yu-Malu's demands, and we've got to do something about it. Make no mistake. She'll do what she threatens unless we can find a way of stopping her."

"Her demands are impossible! If they were complied with three thousand and fifty million people would practically be at the mercy of China...."

"Which is exactly what she wants. We've got to try and stop her."

"The woman's a menace!" exclaimed the high official, stating the obvious, a habit of the majority of high officials. "Look what happened at the Cabinet meeting. All the gold in their watches—grey dust. It's unprecedented."

"The sale of the Crown of the Incas takes place tomorrow afternoon," said Race. "Yu-Malu will carry out her threatened demonstration...."

"I still can't believe it," muttered the high official, shaking his head. "How the devil can she do it?"

"Yu-Malu has resources that we never dreamed of," retorted Race. "But this sale at Sotheby's gives us an opportunity of catching her. I'll bet anything you like that she'll be there in person."

The high official picked up a printed sheet from his desk.

"She won't get away with anything in face of these precautions," he said emphatically,

Race glanced down the sheet. "H'm, there's nothing much more you could do, I'll admit that. Let's hope it'll be effective."

* * * * * * *

Peter Dale raised himself on his elbows above the girl with the auburn hair but she twined her bare arms round his neck and pulled him down. Her large violet eyes were misty, and her breath came quickly and jerkily.

"Interval," he said. "I want a cigarette."

Gently, he extricated himself from her embrace and slid down beside her. Reaching out to the bedside table he took a cigarette from the box on it, put it between his lips, and lit it. Drawing in a lungful of smoke he exhaled slowly.

"Want one?" he asked.

She nodded. He took another cigarette, lit it, and gave it to her. For a while they lay side by side, smoking. The tide of passion that had submerged her was ebbing. Through half-closed eyes he looked at the lovely body, which she made no effort to conceal. He felt a little pang of distaste for what he had planned to do. But it was the only way....

"This is a pretty wonderful place you've got here, isn't it?" he said presently, playing with a tress of the dark auburn hair that curled on her white shoulders. "Aren't you afraid it might get raided?"

The beautifully shaped lips curled contemptuously. The soft mistiness of the eyes had faded. They were hard.

"There's no chance of that," she answered.

"Why?"

"Why do you want to know? It makes no difference to you...."

"I just wondered." He was elaborately casual.

"Is there a railway under us?" he asked. "I heard a sort of rumbling...."

"We often hear that," she said. "This is a volcanic island, or was. It's not marked on any map—that's why I said there was no chance of any strangers coming here...."

She leaned across him and stubbed out her cigarette

in the ashtray on the table. Her hair, soft and perfumed, fell across his face. Her mouth found his and fastened there, opening in a long passionate kiss. He flung away the end of his cigarette and slid his arms round her shoulders. As she slowly settled back, drawing him with her, he moved his hands and smoothed back her hair. He plunged his mouth down on hens, and his questing hands found the carotid arteries on either side of her throat....

* * * * * * *

Bond Street presented an unusual scene on the day when the Crown of the Incas was to be auctioned at Sotheby's. Military barriers had been erected at the Oxford Street and Piccadilly ends of the famous street and the street itself was lined with armed troops and police. The troops faced outwards, as they might have if there was danger of the assassination of some visiting foreign dictator.

On the roof of the B.B.C.'s Aeolian Hall that faced Sotheby's Salerooms, machine guns had been mounted covering the whole area. Television cameras had been set up at strategic points. Every precaution had been taken. Traffic, so far as possible had been diverted, and vehicles that had business in the street were only admitted past the barriers if they bore a special Home Office pass on the windscreens.

Anthony Race inspected the arrangements and declared himself satisfied. That is to say, he was satisfied with the precautions that had been taken. But he was by no means satisfied that they would stop Yu-Malu. The Dragon Princess was no fool. She would have realized that the worldwide publicity given to her threat, and the demands that had followed it, would result in just such precautions being taken, and her plans must have allowed for them.

The Crown of the Incas was not the only *objet vertu* that was being put up for auction that afternoon, but it was by far the most interesting and valuable. Dating back to the year 1593 few, if any, of all the crowns in the world can equal in dignity, in beauty, in grandeur and in value the crown that the Spanish conquerors of Peru made for the statue of Our Lady. Consisting of more than one hundred pounds of the purest gold, set with a total of four hundred and fifty-three emeralds, the crown took six years to complete. The design is so intricate that it challenges belief, the workmanship so delicate that modem jewellers view it with amazement. It was made in a day when time was no object, when craftsmanship was more important than the wage packet, when things of beauty were created as a labour of love.

It was this priceless object that Yu-Malu had threatened to destroy as a demonstration of her power.

Inside Sotheby's, the Chairman had arranged his own precautions. Imperturbable as ever, he was sceptical that anything could happen. But he was not going to take any chances. The auction room was filled by picked security guards, unobtrusive men who mixed with the public, and looked like prosperous buyers.

As the time drew near for the sale to begin, a buzz of conversation filled the big room. It was crowded.

Outside, in Bond Street, there was a larger crowd all waiting to see what would happen. They were an orderly crowd, facing the wooden-faced, expressionless lines of soldiers for the most part in expectant silence.

It was exactly at three-thirty, the time was remembered afterwards, that the ambulance came slowly along the street from the Piccadilly end. It was driven by an elderly woman in a neat blue uniform, and it bore across the windscreen the Home Office permit.

It drew up outside Sotheby's, and was immediately inspected by the officer in charge of the guard. After a short conversation with a woman in the uniform of a hospital nurse, he nodded. The doors at the rear of the ambulance were opened and a very old man in a wheelchair was carefully lowered to the ground by two other nurses with the help of a severe-looking sister.

With great care she wheeled the invalid into Sotheby's. Here she was questioned by the two officials on the doors, but apparently everything was in order and she was allowed to wheel her charge into the auction room.

In the meanwhile, the doors of the ambulance were closed, and it was carefully backed into a space cleared for it by a sergeant of police.

The excitement inside Sotheby's was reaching fever heat, as the elderly sister wheeled the chair containing the old man to a space that was allotted to her.

The next item on the programme was the famous Crown of the Incas.

There was a sudden hush in the great room, which had witnessed so many dramatic moments. The auctioneer cleared his throat and took a sip of water as two attendants brought the fabulous piece of jewellery and placed it carefully on the rostrum.

"Now, ladies and gentlemen," began the auctioneer, "we come to this remarkable and most beautiful piece of historic jewellery, the Crown of the Incas. Apart from its intrinsic value, the exquisite workmanship excels in beauty, in grandeur, in age, in distinction, most of the royal crowns of Europe. In fact, with the possible exception of the crown of the Russian Tsar, which passed into the hands of the Soviet, it is the most valuable crown in the world.

"If you consult your programmes you will find, ladies and gentlemen, a précis of its history.... Will anyone start the bidding at £500,000?"

The bidding went briskly, interrupted by international telephone calls with counter-bids, which were passed up to the auctioneer. At £2,500,000 the bidding slackened. Then it went to £2,600,000 and the auctioneer decided that he had reached the limit—well past the reserve price, which had been put upon the jewel.

"Any advance on £2,600,000?" He glanced swiftly round for some sign, received none, and raised his gavel. "Well, at £2,600,000...."

And then it happened.

The Crown of the Incas dissolved suddenly in front of all of them. It collapsed almost slowly until there was only a heap of emeralds in a small pile of grey dust.

CHAPTER NINE

Never in the sedate history of Sotheby's had the famous auction rooms witnessed such an upheaval as that which followed the sudden disintegration of the Crown of the Incas. The auctioneer, for once in his life speechless, glared at the grey dust strewn over the rostrum, out of which winked little glints of green from the emeralds that were still intact. Clamouring round him, all speaking at once, were the crowd from the body of the room, surging and pressing in their efforts to get a closer view of the catastrophe.

An American collector was spitting out grey dust from his mouth, all that was left of his gold teeth; and several other people were bewailing the fact that their gold watches no longer existed but had been reduced to a few brass wheels and springs.

At the back of the crowd, unnoticed because the entire interest of everybody present was concentrated up at the rostrum, the severe-looking sister wheeled her charge quickly to the exit and out into Bond Street.

The news of what had happened inside had not yet leaked out. Quickly she pushed the wheeled chair to the waiting ambulance, which already had its doors open in readiness. Up the sloping runway, she pushed the chair with its aged occupant, helped by the nurses inside the vehicle. Before anyone knew what had taken place in the auction rooms, the ambulance was away.

As it came out into Oxford Street with bell clanging urgently, the severe-looking sister removed her wig and uniform. The elderly 'gentleman' got out of the wheel-chair and turned miraculously into a smiling and very lovely girl. The two 'nurses' by the strange looking machine that had been concealed by the double bunks, looked questioningly at the Dragon Princess.

"Did it work?"

Yu-Malu nodded as she slipped into a shabby dress and pulled an old hat over her hair.

"Like a charm."

She laughed her silvery laugh, and the Dragonflies joined in.

"Turn into a side street," she ordered, adjusting a pair of spectacles over her eyes. "I'll drop off. You can drive on to the warehouse and dispose of the ambulance. Change out of those uniforms and transfer the machine to the baker's van. I'll meet you at the farm. As soon as you get there we take off for headquarters. Hurry!"

The ambulance swung into a side street. As it slowed, Yu-Malu dropped lightly down and walked quickly away.

The first part of her plan had been successful. The second part she would put into operation when she reached the island.

But it wasn't going to be quite as easy as she expected....

* * * * * * *

There is an unsalubrious part of London that runs erratically following the winding course of the Thames from Wapping to Woolwich. Through Rotherhithe, past the Surrey Commercial Docks, along Limehouse Reach, past Poplar and the West India Docks, is a squalid neighbourhood, the very names that make up its various sections set fire to the imagination and conjure up all kinds of romantic and sinister pictures.

Perhaps in the past there was justification for coupling this neighbourhood with crime, the peddling of dope, opium dens, and the white slave traffic. Legends, fostered by fiction writers, but some of them true enough, sprang up in their hundreds concerning Pennyfields, which is Limehouse, and its Chinese population. In actual fact, as the police will vouch for, this was, and is, the most respectable portion of London. The Chinese are clean, neat, and law-abiding, with the exception of a very small minority.

If you want squalor, cruelty, violence, crime in its most hideous guise, you must look for it in the environs of Deptford only a stone's throw away.

Close to Stepney Station, in a narrow street that runs down to the river at Limehouse Reach, stands a tallish house of crumbling stone and brick. It looks tall only by comparison with the houses near it, which are small. This particular house is one storey higher. The lower floor is a shop that sells all kinds of junk. The window is filled with old books, plates, teacups, vases, plaster figures, etc., mostly in a bad state of repair.

If, however, you succeed in passing the heavy door beside the window, which leads to the house, which you will not do unless you are a very privileged person, you will discover a very different environment. Once you have climbed the narrow stairs and passed a second door at the top there is taste and luxury, thickly woven carpets, hand-made and nearly priceless, cover the floors. The furniture is of period lacquer and the ivory carvings and porcelain vases and figurines are all collectors' pieces.

This is the London home of Tu Li Chang, present head of the Hung Brotherhood, a tall, elderly Chinaman who is seldom seen by any of the inhabitants of the street. A young Chinese who lives on the ground floor behind the shop is generally supposed to be the owner of the whole premises.

To this house came Yu-Malu.

She was in the shabby dress she had put on before leaving the ambulance and she passed without comment by the equally shabby denizens of the narrow street.

Entering the shop door, which set a bell jangling somewhere in the back of the premises, she waited until the young Chinaman appeared through the bamboo curtains that separated the shop from the rooms at the rear.

"Yes?" he asked inquiringly.

Yu-Malu slipped off her shabby glove and showed

him the ring on her finger. He bowed low.

"You will deign to honour my humble abode by passing through on your way to the upper places, your Highness?"

Yu-Malu thanked him graciously and followed him through the bamboo curtains to a plainly furnished, but spotlessly clean, room beyond. Crossing this austere apartment to a door on the opposite side they came out into the shabby hall. Mounting the staircase, the young Chinaman stopped at the door that barred further progress. There was a rusty nail protruding from the frame and this he twisted slightly.

There was a pause and then the door opened revealing the exquisitely furnished hall beyond. It had been opened by a tall Chinaman, dressed in Oriental fashion. A robe of beautifully embroidered silk of a golden yellow draped his lean form and on his head he wore the black hat of a mandarin with a yellow button surmounting the crown. On his hand was a similar ring to that worn by Yu-Malu.

He greeted Yu-Malu with surprised pleasure but without the extreme deference that was usually accorded to her by others.

Tu Li Chang was of royal blood, descended from a long line of ancestors whose origins were lost in the mists of time. He and Yu-Malu were equals and as such they treated each other.

"You are welcome to my unworthy abode, your Highness," he said in the gutteral tones of his race, slightly stressing his sibilants. "To what am I indebted for this most unexpected joy?"

While speaking he had conducted her into a large room of great elegance and beauty, and pulled forward a chair.

"I have just struck my first blow against the West," answered the Dragon Princess. She sat down in a soft cushioned chair, looking incongruous in her shabby dress among that luxurious setting. "I must be returning to my island headquarters at once but while I was in London I decided to call on you and acquaint you with what I have accomplished."

She told him what she had done and he listened with grave attention. When she had finished he nodded slowly.

"You have done well, your Highness," he said. "We of the Hung Brotherhood, of which I am but an unworthy member, are sure that the future of our beloved China is safe in your keeping. You will restore its greatness and its grandeur, even greater than it was in the past. This has been given to you as your destiny."

"I shall carry it out," said Yu-Malu with conviction. "Have no fear. However long it may take I shall achieve our long cherished desire."

She took out her cigarette case and helped herself to one of her rose-tipped cigarettes. Tu Li Chang courteously held out a gold lighter into the flame of which she dipped the end of the cigarette.

"There is something else, your Highness," he said. "You have not honoured me with your presence entirely to inform me of this gold campaign?"

Yu-Malu let a thin stream of smoke escape from her lips.

"I want your help," she said.

"You have it—mine and the help of all those who belong to the Triad."

"There is a man who is becoming a nuisance to me. His name is Anthony Race. I want him—removed."

"That should be a simple matter, your Highness," murmured Tu Li Chang. "I will give my attention to this trivial business. You will take tea?"

"It would give me great pleasure," said Yu-Malu.

Tu Li Chang struck a gong and a Chinese girl appeared almost before the vibrations had faded away. Tu Li Chang spoke to her in Chinese and she bowed low and hurried away.

"Do not give any more thought to this man, Race," said Tu Li Chang. "From this moment he has ceased to exist."

* * * * * * *

Anthony Race lived in a small service flat near Westminster. It consisted of three rooms, none of them very large, and a microscopic kitchen. There was a bathroom in which it was possible, with a certain amount of ingenuity, to squeeze into.

Race had many times decided to move into a larger and more comfortable flat, but he had never got beyond the stage of thinking about it.

After a long session with the high treasury official the chaotic happening at Sotheby's he had snatched a hasty meal and, feeling completely exhausted from a plethora of talk and argument, had driven back to his flat. He wanted a quiet evening with a book and a drink, a short period during which he could forget Yu-Malu, Treasury officials, and everything connected with his workaday life. It would give him time to recoup his strength and lessen the nervous tension from which he was suffering.

Although his sitting room was small it was comfortable. A large studio couch was drawn up in front of the electric fire, there was a bookcase full of books, a large easy chair and a sideboard containing drinks.

Race had a hot bath, put on a dressing gown, and pouring himself out a large whisky and water, settled down on the couch with a book that he had been wanting to read for some time.

It was quite early and he looked forward to a long, pleasant evening, undisturbed, followed by bed and a long sleep.

But it didn't happen like that!

First of all he couldn't help his mind straying from the book to Katrina and Peter Dale. He tried to put them out of his mind. He told himself that thinking about them wouldn't do any good. Action was the only thing that would help them, and action was impossible without further facts concerning the whereabouts of the place to which they had been taken.

He gave up trying to read at last and switched on the television. He stuck out an alleged comedy series, waiting for the play that was to follow. When it did it proved to be a sordid drama set in a back street slum concerning a group of people so uninteresting that he couldn't care what happened to any of them.

He switched over to another channel. Here was a so-called spectacular. The setting looked like something that an idiot child might have made from a box of Meccano. A ragged lot of dancers cavorted before this without rhyme or apparent reason—certainly without melody—and these were followed by a girl who sang through her nose and looked like a kitchen mop that had just been washed.

Race turned off the television in disgust. He wondered what people thought was really entertainment these days and decided that quite obviously they didn't think at all!

He went out into the kitchen and made himself some coffee. Carrying this back into the sitting room he lit a cigarette and settled back on the studio couch. He felt dog-tired but knew that if he went to bed he wouldn't sleep. He had experienced this kind of thing before. It meant that his nerves were jangling from strain. The thing to do was a long walk in the country—twenty or thirty miles—a hot bath followed by hot whisky and bed. A certain cure. In the morning one would feel like pushing a bus over. But he wasn't in the country and, even if he were, he hadn't the time to spare.

There was nothing for it but to go to bed. He finished the coffee, brushed his teeth, and got into bed. For a long time he lay awake, tossing from side to side, but at last he fell into a fitful sleep...

He never knew what it was that woke him. Some slight sound that had percolated through to his brain. But he knew what it meant.

There was someone in the flat!

They were in the adjoining room.

Race slipped noiselessly out of bed and moved over to the door. He listened. He could hear the faint sound of movement from the other side of the closed door. There was undoubtedly someone in the sitting room and he wondered what was the best thing to do. Should he go out to the intruder or wait for the intruder to come to him?

He decided that he would wait for the intruder to come to him. There was a switch beside the door. He would wait until the intruder was safely in the bedroom and then switch on the light....

He took up his position beside the door and waited, almost holding his breath.

He heard the handle grasped and gently turned. Very slowly the door began to open. Wider and wider and something slipped through into the room.

Race braced himself. His fingers pressed down the light switch and the centre light came on with a sudden glare. At the same moment Race kicked the door shut, but he was not prepared for what he saw.

Blinking in the sudden glare of light was a Dacoit! He wore nothing but a loincloth and he was oiled from head to toe. In his mouth he carried a wicked- looking knife...

Race had no time for any more detail. The man was

on him, snarling, the knife in his hand. Race caught his wrist as it descended and at the same time cut at his neck with the edge of his hand. The Dacoit grunted, twisted himself free, and crouched for a further attack. Race picked up a chair to defend himself. The Dacoit watched him, still crouched on his haunches. He began to move round in a half circle, watching for an opportunity to spring at Race with the knife.

Race hurled the chair. The Dacoit twisted out of the way with a squirm of his lithe body and sprang at Race. He dropped flat on his face and his attacker passed over him. He turned swiftly, but Race was quicker. He pivoted round on his stomach and caught the Dacoit's ankle. The man gave a grunt and over-balanced, falling heavily beside Race. Race turned over and grabbed at the man, but the oil with which he was covered made it difficult to get a grip on him. He was as elusive as an eel and jumped to his feet. Race was still on the floor. The Dacoit's thin lips curled back from his teeth in a snarl of triumph as he saw his victim at his mercy. He raised the knife and brought it down with all his force towards Race's throat. It was only by a hair that it missed. Race managed to jerk his body out of the way even while the knife was descending. The razor sharp blade swished down and stuck in the floor. Before the Dacoit could pull it out Race thrust at his stomach with both feet. The Dacoit shot backwards, crashing into the bed.

But he had lost his knife!

Race was on his feet, ready for the next attack.

But the Dacoit lacked courage without the knife. He leaped up and dashed for the door into the sitting room. Race went after him. He caught the man as he was making for the kitchen. The Dacoit swung a vicious blow at his face but Race dodged it and landed a beautiful uppercut to the man's chin.

The Dacoit's head jerked back and he staggered. But he recovered before Race could take advantage of his adversary. He kicked out catching Race full in the stomach and doubling him up. The Dacoit was through the kitchen door in a flash. The window through which he had come was open and he dived out on to the fire escape that ran up the back of the flats.

Like a giant black spider he sped down the iron ladder and by the time Race had reached the window he had reached the ground. He disappeared round the side of the building and after a moment Race heard the sound of a car driving away.

Shakily he went back to the sitting room and poured himself a stiff whisky.

The intruder had been brought to the flat that night and there was little doubt in Race's mind who was responsible.

Yu-Malu.

At that moment, in a closed car that was speeding eastward, the Dacoit was explaining in his own language to an unsympathetic Chinaman why he had failed to carry out his mission.

* * * * * * *

Peter Dale looked down at the auburn-haired Dragonfly on his bed. She was quite unconscious. It had only required a comparatively slight pressure on the two carotid arteries one on each side of her throat, to do the trick. She had scarcely had time to realize what was happening before she passed out.

But she wouldn't remain like that for long. He pulled one of the sheets off the bed and tore it into wide strips. With these he bound her legs, pulled her arms down beside her body and bound them there. By the time he had finished she looked rather like an Egyptian mummy but she was quite helpless. He finished the job by securely gagging her. He felt rather mean at treating her like this but consoled himself, with the certainty that she would not have had any compunction in treating him a great deal worse, if it had suited her.

By the time he had finished she was beginning to show signs of returning consciousness. But he had plenty of time. No one would be coming to disturb him until the dwarf brought in his breakfast. Which left him most of the night.

He lit a cigarette.

He had watched how the other Dragonflies had opened the door when they had left in the morning, and he searched the filmy negligée that the girl had worn when she came in. He found what he was seeking in a tiny pocket. It was a small silver whistle.

The sound it emitted was inaudible to the human ear, but when it was blown it acted on some kind of electronic device that released the lock of the door.

A sound from the bed made him turn. The girl was twisting her body, trying to get free. She had recovered her senses and her large eyes glared up at him malignantly.

"I'm sorry to have to do this to you, my dear," said Peter. "Please accept my apologies for the indignity and for curtailing the night's enjoyment."

The hatred in her eyes deepened and she uttered a string of unintelligible sounds.

"I'm going to leave you now. I should try to get a little sleep."

He put the whistle to his lips and blew. There was no sound but he heard the sharp 'click' as the mechanism operating the lock worked.

The question now was—was there a guard outside? Cautiously, he slid back the door. The corridor beyond was brilliantly lighted, but appeared to be deserted.

Peter closed the door and blew once again on the tiny whistle. Again there was a sharp click. The door was locked once more.

So far so good.

He stood, pressed up against the wall, and listened. Everything was silent. He tried to get his bearings. He wasn't sure which direction he ought to take. The corridor stretched away, a broad, white lane, to left and right. At each end it was intersected by two others. Along the wall, on the same side as his own, were other doors. He had slipped on a pair of trousers and a shirt, but his feet were bare. Making no sound, his senses alert for any sound, he crept to the end of the right-hand corridor.

When he reached the intersecting corridor, he paused. It was similar in appearance to the other except that there appeared to be no doors. Instead the walls were lined with glass, behind which queer shapes moved, nightmare shapes of strange insects.

There seemed to be dozens of these white passages, and it wasn't long before he realized that he was lost. He tried to remember the location of the radio room from what the Dragonfly had told him, but he couldn't.

She had not given him any details—only the general direction. He hadn't dared to question her in case she should have become suspicious.

There was an archway—he remembered that. She had mentioned an archway....

He hadn't seen any archway so far. The glass-walled corridors, with their fish and tropical plants and hideous reptiles, were all smooth.

He went on again and, presently, just when he was beginning to feel that he had had all his trouble for nothing, he came upon an archway supporting the roof.

But there was no sign of the radio room.

There was no sign of any room.

Peter stopped and glanced at his wristwatch. It was four o'clock. He had been wandering about this underground labyrinth for over two hours.

Well, at least he had found an archway. What was the next move?

Even if he succeeded in finding the radio room, he would have to be careful. He hadn't seen or heard any sounds of life during his exploration, but there was bound to be someone on duty in the radio room. Somebody, surely was on duty night and day.

He felt very tired and leaned against the supporting buttress of the arch. It wouldn't be long before the inhabitants of the place would be stirring and his chance of getting a message out would be gone. To have got so far and fail....

And then he saw the two little buttons set in the concrete arch against which he was leaning. What could they be for? He hesitated. If he pressed one or both anything might happen. They might work an alarm signal. On the other hand they might control the entrance to the place he was seeking.

Well, nothing venture nothing gain. He pressed the top one. Instantly the floor near his feet slid back. He peered down. He could hear from below the faint hum of an electric generator. He moved cautiously down the steps and came to the door marked 'Danger' which Katrina had found.

It was partly open and the humming of the generator was louder. He approached the door, making no sound in his naked feet. Very gently he pushed it farther open and peered round the edge. He was looking into a brilliantly lighted room and knew that he had reached his objective.

The radio installation!

He slid round the door. The room was empty. If there had been anyone on duty they had left. Was that the reason for the door being ajar? If so, they might return at any minute. He had better make the most of his opportunity.

He closed the heavy door. There was a steel bar on the inside that fitted into a socket. He lifted it into place. The door was secure from the inside. If anyone came they would have difficulty in getting in.

Quickly he went over and inspected the racks of instruments. This was the transmitter. He pulled down a large switch and a red light glowed on the control panel. He put on a pair of headphones that lay on the bench and slowly turned the dial that would give him the wavelength of the receiver at British Intelligence....

* * * * * *

Yu-Malu's specially fitted private plane began its long descent towards the island under the skilful hand of the Dragonfly pilot.

It had made the journey in record time, flying high above the clouds. The farm from which they had taken off belonged to a member of the Triad, as did the warehouse in which they had stored the ambulance. Yu-Malu had similar ports of call in nearly every country in the world, places where she could rely on any assistance that she required, all owned by members of the far-reaching 'Hung Society', which had its branches everywhere.

She had changed before leaving for her island headquarters and was once more her immaculate and lovely self.

She was well-satisfied with the results of her trip.

She had successfully carried out her demonstration at Sotheby's and delivered her demands through the medium of Sir Basil Samuels' speech. The insertion of these demands in his speech had been effected by another member of the Triad, and she was aware of Sir Basil's little peculiarities. He would read what lay before him without being cognisant of what he said.

And he had.

She laughed as she thought how easy it had all been. These self-satisfied people of the West were stupid—so excessively stupid. They were only fit for slaves.

"I cannot get any signal from the island, your Highness," said the girl at the radio control. "I have been sending out the usual 'stand-by for landing' signal but there's no reply...."

Yu-Malu frowned.

"D.18 should be on duty," she said. "Turn on the television."

The Dragonfly obeyed. In a few seconds the small screen became illuminated.

"Tune into the radio room," ordered Yu-Malu.

The screen flickered, Lights flashed across it, and then a hazy picture began to form. It grew clearer and the Dragon Princess uttered an angry exclamation,

"It's that man, Dale!" she snapped. "He's got into the radio room and he's operating the transmitter. Sound the automatic alarm."

The girl at the radio control pulled down a switch and turned a knob. The radio beam went out from the plane, which would operate alarm signals throughout the island headquarters.

"Make all speed to land," cried Yu-Malu. "Somebody will suffer for this...."

The plane dived steeply, rushing towards the island under full power. It was a dangerous expedient, but the Dragonfly at the control handled the craft superbly and coolly. At exactly the right moment she shut off the power and glided down to the landing strip, touching down with scarcely a jar....

The alarms were jangling everywhere as Yu-Malu hurried through the corridors towards the radio room. Sleepy eyed, half-dressed, Dragonflies were running about, intermixed with the rest of the staff. They clamoured round Yu-Malu as soon as they caught sight of her, asking what the trouble was.

Without pausing she explained briefly, and they all followed her towards the radio room. On the way, Sin Wu appeared.

"Your Highness. I did not know you were back. I should have been in the cavern to greet you. Why are the alarms...?"

"Dale has got into the radio room. Come quickly—all of you!"

"Look!" exclaimed Sin Wu when they reached the arch. "The floor is open...."

Yu-Malu was already down the steps. She reached the door marked 'danger' and tried to open it. But it was fast.

"He has put the bar up on the inside," said the Dragon Princess. "Fetch the metal cutter."

She waited impatiently until two men returned with an oxyacetylene apparatus and started to cut through the thick steel. The flame bit into the metal cutting through it like a hot knife through butter.

Peter Dale turned from the transmitter as the door crashed open.

"You are too late," he began, but that's all he said.

Yu-Malu, her lovely face twisted into a mask of devilish hate, shot him three times in the stomach.

CHAPTER TEN

The radio message received at the headquarters of British Intelligence from Peter Dale before he died, writhing in agony, from the bullets in his stomach fired by Yu-Malu, was passed on to Anthony Race.

"A volcanic island—somewhere," said Race, disappointedly. "It's something to have heard at all, I suppose, but it's like looking for a needle in a haystack...."

"Did he mention anything about Katrina?" asked the friend he was speaking to.

Race shook his head.

"No, unfortunately. The chap who took the message said Dale was a bit incoherent and in a desperate hurry."

He went round to the Treasury to report this latest development to the high official. That individual received the. news with as much excitement as high officials are permitted.

"We must find this island," he insisted. "We must co-opt the Services...."

"I don't see what good the Army's going to be...."

"Naturally, I was referring to the Navy," interrupted the high official with dignity, "and possibly the Air Force...."

"We might be able to locate the place by taking cross-bearings from the waves transmitted from their radio installation—on a similar principle to the television detector vans," suggested Race. "The transmitter must be a very powerful one...."

"An excellent idea!" agreed the high official. "Get on to it at once—at once! There is no time to be lost!"

"I realize that. If Yu-Malu's demands are ignored she will carry out the next part of her programme—the destruction of the gold reserves...."

"Such a possibility is unthinkable!" declared the high official emphatically. "No stone must be left unturned, every avenue must be explored...!"

Race left him muttering clichés and went to consult a radio expert. He was in the middle of this when Yu-Malu's message reached him....

* * * * * * *

Yu-Malu had no idea exactly what message Peter Dale had managed to get through to London before she had shot him. It was doubtful if he had been able to give the location of her island headquarters, but he might have been able to say enough to start them searching...

She decided to revise her plans to deal with the situation. Katrina, recovering from the shock of her ordeal in the room of 'The Seventh Beatitude' was still a prisoner. The Dragon Princess decided that she could be made use of.

She transmitted a message herself.

It was brief and to the point.

She stated that she held Katrina Evans a prisoner and the girl would be killed if any steps were taken to thwart her plans. She would be prepared, however, to negotiate with someone in authority, provided that she was guaranteed safe custody and that no attempt was made to arrest or detain her. The representative must have full powers to deal with her demands. She suggests that a rendezvous should be arranged to meet her, in person, in the restaurant of the Post Office Tower at noon on the following day. An acceptance of this plan must be broadcast on all wavelengths of the B.B.C. within the next two hours. If her ultimatum is ignored, one of Katrina's hands will be cut off at the wrist and sent to the British Government.

"You will be taking a very great risk, your Highness," said Sin Wu, shaking his head doubtfully. "These people may not regard their given word as inviolate. Our Chinese code of honour is not theirs. You could run into extreme danger...."

"Do not worry, Sin Wu," answered Yu-Malu. "I shall take every precaution. See that the plane is ready and waiting."

The high official at the Treasury was aghast when Race informed him what Yu-Malu had said.

"It's preposterous, unheard of!" he expostulated. "We cannot negotiate with this woman. The Government would never agree. The Prime Minister...."

"The Government will have to!" snapped Race curtly. "This is our chance to get hold of Yu-Malu. It's a case of the fly walking into the spider's parlour."

"That's all very well...," began the high official.

"With the co-operation of the Admiralty I expect to get the location of this island pretty soon. Their experts are working on it now. They expect to come up with the information we require within the next twelve hours. While Yu-Malu is 'negotiating' at the Post Office Tower, we can be arranging to raid her island headquarters! This menace to civilization can be scotched for good!"

The high official argued and Race argued. At last the high official got through to Downing Street. Race paced impatiently up and down the office while the high official talked and talked. Eventually, the high official put down the telephone.

"The Prime Minister wants to see you," he said.

Race broke all speed records to Downing Street. He had less than an hour to get the Government's permission and give the go ahead to the B.B.C. and other major broadcasters to put the acceptance of Yu-Malu's plan on the air.

He managed it with just ten minutes to spare.

And now he had to make his own preparations for the meeting with the Dragon Princess. This time, he thought, she had overreached herself, this time she was not going to get away so easily....

* * * * * * *

Katrina had been told of the fate that had overtaken Peter Dale. Yu-Malu had taken a sadistic pleasure in informing her herself.

"You will be wise," she said, "if you adhere to your oath of allegiance to my service. Any attempt to escape will be met by instant death—and it will not be a pleasant death. Take heed of what I say."

Katrina was left alone to think over what she had said. Although she was a prisoner in the sense that there were certain parts of the underground labyrinth barred to her, she was not confined to the room that had been allotted to her. She was expected to take part in the duties shared by the other Dragonflies, in the general smooth running of the Dragon Princess's headquarters. 'D.1' was the Dragonfly in charge of operations. From her the rest received their instructions—except on special assignments when they came from Yu-Malu herself.

There was a well-appointed restaurant where the Dragonflies took their meals. The cooking was excellent, served by male waiters who were all Chinese. This was reserved entirely for the Dragonflies. The actual staff ate in a separate canteen, and Yu-Malu was served by a very full and efficient staff. Engineers, electricians, carpenters, painters, every trade and profession had its representative, and the entire vast organisation ran like a well-oiled machine.

A number of ventilating shafts, communicating with the outside air, kept the atmosphere clean, cool, and fresh. There were only two means of reaching the island above, by means of the giant lift in the cavern, and another, private lift, in Yu-Malu's own apartment suite. But few of the inhabitants ever left their under-ground home, except when they went on expedition with Yu-Malu.

Katrina discovered that there was a vast cold storage containing enough food for several months and that this was periodically replenished by expeditions to the mainland in a fast motor yacht that was kept in a concealed mooring on the leeward side of the island.

Rather to her surprise she found that the Dragonflies were only too willing to extol the amenities of their home. They were proud to tell her and, in some cases to show her, how well it had been designed and fitted.

It must, she thought, have taken many months, if not years, of intensive work by gangs of experts to achieve these results, and she marvelled again at the organising genius of Yu-Malu.

The first time she heard the low rumbling in the bowels of the earth she was a little frightened, but the Dragonflies assured her that it often happened. It was nothing to worry about.

In spite of the Dragon Princess's warning, Katrina was determined at the first opportunity to find a way of getting out of her predicament. She guessed that Peter Dale, before he had been shot down, had succeeded in getting some kind of message through, and that meant that Anthony Race would be using every endeavour to find the island. If he succeeded, she would stand a much better chance if she were above ground instead of being cooped up underground. She would not only be able to see what was going on but there would be a better chance of being able to hide.

The cavern had been put out of bounds to her. The only other way to the open air was the lift in Yu-Malu's private suite.

Would there be a chance of her being able to use it?

She had heard from one of the Dragonflies that Yu-Malu was going away that day. There might just possibly be a chance if she could take advantage of this. The first thing to do was to get into the Dragon Princess's apartment. And this wasn't going to be so easy.

But luck was suddenly to come down heavily on her side. Unexpectedly, the way opened for her....

* * * * * * *

By eleven o'clock on the morning that Yu-Malu was due to keep her appointment with Anthony Race; all his arrangements for her reception had been completed. Not only this but he had received news from the Admiralty that the position of the island had been located. They had, using an intricate system of cross-bearings based on Yu-Malu's own transmission, succeeded in pinpointing her headquarters.

A flotilla of the Mediterranean Fleet was ready and awaiting orders to sail for the island which, although not marked on any maritime chart, the Admiralty considered to be the result of the last time Mount Etna erupted. A similar island was formed during a volcanic eruption off Iceland, and it was their belief that this unknown island, which Yu-Malu was using was the result of the same kind of natural phenomena.

Getting the necessary authority for the use of the Navy, and checking all the numerous details for the proposed raid, had occupied quite a lot of time, and Race was unable to set off for his rendezvous with the Dragon Princess until nearly half-past eleven. Still, half an hour, he thought, would give him plenty of time. All the security arrangements at the Post Office Tower were in hand and should be ready.

To his annoyance, however, he was held up near Broadcasting House. The street was blocked with people watching the Press photographers taking pictures of a helicopter standing near the kerb. An outside television broadcast unit was also taking pictures and adding to the confusion.

Fuming with impatience at the delay, Race called a harassed sergeant of police and demanded to know what was happening.

"It's this exhibition, sir," explained the man.

"What exhibition?"

"The British Executive Travel Association, sir, at St. George's Hotel. They've got a stunt on. That helicopter is supposed to have been 'booked' by a traffic warden for 'parking' on an overtime parking meter. It'll be some time before the road's clear. Where do you want to get to, sir?"

"The Post Office Tower."

"You'd best cut through that side street, sir...."

The sergeant gave directions, and Race, cursing all and sundry for the day, followed them as quickly as he could. By the time he arrived at the Tower, he only had five minutes to spare before Yu-Malu was due.

When he reached the restaurant, he found that it was fairly full. A number of attractive girl were chattering and laughing over an early lunch, and there was a smattering of sightseers, people on holiday who had come to see enjoy the wonderful view that stretched away in all directions.

There was no sign, as yet, of Yu-Malu. Race glanced at his watch. It was three minutes to noon. Hastily he carried out a final check on his arrangements. A table had been reserved for him, and he saw that a number of security men acting as restaurant staff were at their posts.

All that was wanting was—Yu-Malu.

Would she keep the appointment? After all, it had been made at her own suggestion. But she might realize the risk she would be running and cry off at the last moment.

Race watched the hands of his watch creep nearer and nearer to twelve.

A clock began to chime the quarters and then to strike the hour. Noon.

Precisely as the last stroke of the hour faded to silence, Yu-Malu entered the restaurant.

She was a vision of loveliness. Exquisitely dressed and coiffured, she stood for a moment just within the entrance and looked coolly round, the eyes of everyone in the restaurant staring at her in open admiration.

Race came quickly over to her and bowed.

"I have a table reserved for us," he said. "Allow me to escort you over to it."

She nodded graciously and followed him over to the table. The headwaiter pulled out a chair for her and she sat down. Race took the chair facing her. The head-waiter bent slightly forward.

"Will you order now, sir?" he inquired deferentially.

"Later." It was Yu-Malu who answered.

The headwaiter inclined his head and withdrew. Yu-Malu took her jewelled cigarette case from her handbag, took out one of her tiny, petal-tipped ciga-rettes, and accepted the light that Race held out to her.

"Now," she said briskly, blowing out a thin, grey cloud of smoke, "give me the formula for the cold rocket fuel."

Race was a little taken aback.

"You don't believe in wasting time, do you?" he said.

"I do not, Mr. Race," retorted Yu-Malu. "I'm not here for pleasure. I want the formula in exchange for the safety of Katrina Evans. I am prepared, for the moment, to wait for the other items in my ultimatum. I made this very clear when I arranged this meeting...."

"I didn't expect that you'd be in such a hurry," he said, stalling for time.

"Why not?" she demanded.

"Well, it's usual to take these things at a more leisurely pace...."

"Mr. Race," she interrupted, "I am a busy woman. I have neither the time nor the inclination to adopt your absurd Western habits of diplomacy."

"I always understood," said Race with a smile that flickered round his thin mouth for a brief second, "that the Chinese were very deliberate in their methods of bargaining?"

"The Chinese," she replied, "like all sensible people, suit the method to the occasion. This occasion requires speed."

"I have not come prepared to...," he began, and she broke in before he could complete the sentence.

"Then you have not kept to your side of the bargain."

"I was about to say that I have not brought the formula with me. I have a document, however, which I am prepared to sign, promising to hand it over to you once Miss Evans is back, safe and sound."

Yu-Malu crushed out the stub of her cigarette in the ashtray.

"Mr. Race, I have given my word that Miss Evans will remain unharmed. Our code of honour in China is inviolate. I have never yet broken my word."

Race believed her. Although she was a ruthless adversary he felt rather like a small boy who has been reprimanded for not behaving properly. All the more so since he had, and never had had, any intention of allowing the formula to fall into her hands. The government had been prepared to go so far but no farther....

Her cold, hard eyes were watching him intently. He felt that she was reading his mind like a printed page.

"I think I understand," she said in a voice that was as cold and sharp as chipped ice. "You never had any intention of honouring your word...."

"I never gave my word...."

With a sudden, swift, graceful movement, Yu-Malu rose to her feet.

"There is no point in continuing this interview," she said.

"Not so fast," snapped Race, jumping up and facing her. "You're not leaving as easily as that."

He signalled to the security men and they started to close in but the attractive girls who had been taking an early lunch seemed to have suddenly decided to leave. They clustered round the security men as Yu-Malu twisted the green ring on her finger...

A spray in a fine cloud shot from it, catching Race full in the face. He felt all the power go out of his muscles, collapsing back into his chair.

Swiftly, the Dragon Princess crossed to the exit. The attractive girls—all Dragonflies—saw to it that she had á free path. The security men had succumbed, like Race, to the drug contained in the rings they all wore. Yu-Malu, protected by this rearguard action on the part of her followers, made her way swiftly to one of the observation platforms.

Race, fighting off the effects of the drug, which didn't seem to last very long, came staggering after her.

But he was too late.

He heard the noise of the helicopter as he reached the observation platform. It was circling the Tower and even as he looked, a rope ladder came snaking down from the cockpit. It fell almost at Yu-Malu's feet. As the security men, uncertain from the effects of the drug, and hampered by the clinging Dragonflies, came out on to the platform, the Dragon Princess caught the rope ladder and clinging to it, was swept away, high over London.

The last Race saw of her she was climbing the swaying ladder as the helicopter soared up until it was only a speck in the sky.

CHAPTER ELEVEN

"I ought to have had that damned Air Travel Exhibition checked on," said Anthony Race bitterly to the chief of his security men a few hours later. "The helicopter was only ninety seconds away from here...."

"Do you mean she had it all worked out, sir?"

"She always has everything worked out!" snapped Race.

"We've got those other women...."

"I very much doubt if we shall get anything out of them," said Race dubiously. He felt depressed and a little futile. The Dragon Princess had shown a superior organising power that was very galling, and, what was the most serious thing of all, he had practically signed Katrina's death warrant. Yu-Malu, in her rage at, her plans being thwarted, would wreak her vengeance on Katrina....

Unless the Navy could get there in time.

The flotilla was awaiting orders but they couldn't hope to make as much speed as Yu-Malu who would no doubt be flying.... However, the quicker they started the better. If they weren't in time to save Katrina's life, they could at least avenge her death. He got on to the

Admiralty and explained what had happened. The official to whom he spoke, a sensible man whom the war had taught to act quickly, agreed to radio the orders to sail at once.

"What are you going to do, Race? Ought to go with 'em, you know."

"I'll pick them up on the way, sir. The R.A.F. will fly me out to Sicily—there's a boat standing by for me there."

"Good, good. The best of luck!"

The Dragonflies, after their efforts to assist in Yu-Malu's escape, had proved to be very docile. Race was a little suspicious of this attitude until he realized that they had been trained to accept the inevitable with all the stoicism of the Orient. Nothing was found on them when they were searched that was at all helpful. One of them carried a small transmitter and Race guessed that this was how the helicopter had been signalled. It had puzzled him but, of course, this was the explanation. The girl had sent the signal as soon as she had seen that Yu-Malu was in trouble.

No amount of questioning resulted in any information at all. They remained dumb and completely unaffected by all threats or cajolery.

Race had hoped to get some details about the island from them, but had to give it up as hopeless. They smiled politely in answer to all his questions and said nothing.

It was useless wasting any more time with the Dragonflies. He had already arranged with the R.A.F.

to fly him out to the flotilla, steaming at full speed in the Mediterranean towards the island headquarters of the Dragon Princess. He could only hope that he would get there in time.

Katrina stood in the sunlight and drew in great gulping breaths of pure air.

She had succeeded in getting out of the underground headquarters, and felt a wave of emotion sweep over her as she gazed at the blue sky, the low hills, and the green of the trees and the undergrowth. The air was warm and carried the tang of the sea. For the first few seconds she could only stand and breathe it all in. Although the air conditioning down below was excellent, this was the real thing.

But she had no time to stand about enjoying her freedom. If there should be any of the staff from below lurking about up here, she might be spotted and her freedom would be short-lived.

She had come up in Yu-Malu's private lift, which emerged in the shelter of a shallow cave in the side of a low hill, and the first thing she had done was to send the small lift down again. She hoped that it would not be missed.

She was still amazed at the piece of good luck, which enabled her to escape. She had seized an opportunity that presented itself and it had paid off.

Although Yu-Malu's private apartments were cleaned by part of the male staff, a selected number of the Dragonflies did the light dusting. There were so many exquisite pieces of china and ivory carving that required delicate handling that could not be left to the rougher handling of the male cleaners.

Katrina had been attached to this party and could scarcely believe her good fortune. She hadn't expected that there would be any chance of escaping. That had come completely unexpectedly.

There were half a dozen Dragonflies in the dusting party including herself, and each one had her allotted task so that there was no confusion. She had been given the task of attending to the Dragon Princess's luxurious bedroom in company with another Dragonfly.

She spotted the lift at once. There had been no attempt at concealing it, possibly because there was no need. It was quite a small affair, only large enough for one person, and was set in the wall. The entrance was guarded by a fine gold-meshed grill, through which it was possible to see the control panel inside.

And the sight of that lift caused Katrina's heart to beat faster. If only she could use it. But there wasn't a chance. The Dragonfly with her would give the alarm if she made any attempt to, and the others were within call.

She was dusting and polishing the contents of Yu-Malu's dressing table, a long, low affair of carved ebony, with great mirrors that could be adjusted to any angle, and covered with gold stoppered bottles and jars. There was a set of solid gold brushes and hand mirrors, the backs inlaid with jewels and an exquisite casket to match. Katrina, polishing gently with a soft leather, racked her brains to think of some way by which she could use the lift, but she couldn't. It was exasperating. She might never have another opportunity as good as this, but she dared not take advantage of it....

And then the chance was thrown in her lap.

The Dragonfly with her was dusting the bedhead with its fitments on either side. She finished one side and hurried round to do the other. The floor was covered by an enormous Chinese carpet of silky pile, a lovely thing that must have been worth a small fortune. On each side of the enormous bed was a rug, also of Chinese workmanship, with a thicker, softer pile, into which Yu-Malu's feet could sink when she swung her legs off the bed. Katrina gave a savage tug at the rug. The Dragonfly tripped over and, unable to save herself, fell heavily, striking her head on the carved footboard.

She had given hardly a cry and the soft carpet had completely deadened the sound of her fall. She just lay still with a thin trickle of blood oozing from her forehead.

Katrina was at her side in a second. The girl was unconscious. Now was her chance.

She slipped over to the half-open door, shut it gently and turned the key in the lock.

Praying that the use of the lift wouldn't sound any alarm, she ran over to it and slid back the golden-grill. The next second she was inside, had jerked the grill, which was also the door of the lift, shut, and pressed the control switch.

The lift shot upwards without a sound and a few seconds later, she stepped out into a shallow cave in the hillside—free.

But it wouldn't be long before her absence was discovered. When the Dragonfly recovered her senses she would give the alarm and they would come searching for her.

Her best chance was to make for the wooded hills. Here there would be plenty of cover. How long she would be able to retain her freedom was problematical. She had nothing in the way of food, unless she could find something edible growing on the island. But anything was better than being cooped up in the labyrinth below.

As she ran, stumbling over the rough ground, a tremor shook the earth beneath her feet. It was slight but the whole island seemed to shiver. She was too intent on finding a suitable hiding place to worry much about it. According to what she had heard, these slight shocks often happened.

She clambered up the hillside and at last, tired and panting, she reached the fringe of the wooded crest. The trees grew thickly, their trunks rising out of thick masses of tangled undergrowth. She could hear the sound of the sea breaking gently on the rocky coastline, and the screech of gulls, but otherwise nothing.

When she had penetrated more deeply into the wood, she paused to rest.

How long would it be before they came searching for her? It couldn't be very long. The trees grew so thickly that it was nearly dark in the heart of the wood although the sun was shining brilliantly, and it was terribly hot—a humid heat that seemed to come as much from the earth as from the sunlit sky.

The heavy canopy of branches met overhead, interlacing to form a thick green ceiling through which she could only catch a patch of sky here and there. It gave her an idea.

When she had completely recovered her breath and a little of her strength, she put her idea into execution.

She found a tree that soared away into the green tangle above and began to climb it. It was difficult going. Twice she slipped and almost fell and once a branch broke under her weight and she slithered down several feet before she could check herself, but at last she forced her way through the matted, leaves and branches and found the sky above her.

Her hands were sore and bleeding, but she gritted her teeth and went on a little higher until she was able to wedge herself in the fork of a branch, for the moment, at least, safe.

And she was only just in time.

From below she could hear the sound of voices, calling and shouting.

The hunt for her had started.

Anthony Race stood on the bridge of a British destroyer beside the captain and stared out over the expanse of sea.

Nearby, the other ships of the flotilla steamed at full speed, their white wakes streaming out behind them in the blue-grey water.

The seaplane had come down like a giant gull, transferred him to a fast launch, which had carried him to the destroyer, and then taken off, swung round in a wide and graceful curve, and headed back to the mainland.

"How long before we sight the island, Captain?" asked Race.

The captain, a grizzled man with the deep tan of long hours of sun and salt spray, pursed his lips.

"Couldn't say exactly." He looked at Race curiously. "What's the object, sir?"

"Didn't they tell you?"

The captain shook his head.

"Only that we were to proceed with all speed to this island, sir. I was told to take my instructions from you."

"I see."

"They did mention that there might be a bit of a scrap, sir."

Race took out his cigarette case and helped himself to a cigarette. He offered the case to the captain.

"No, thank you, sir. Only smoke a pipe."

Race put away the case and lit his cigarette. The captain watched him with an expressionless face.

"Have you ever heard of a woman named Yu-Malu?" asked Race.

"Can't say that I have," replied the captain. "Who is she?"

"Surely you must have read the papers?"

"Been to sea, sir, for the past eight weeks."

"Well, she is the woman we are after," said Race. He inhaled deeply and let the smoke trickle from his nostrils. "She is the most dangerous woman in existence...."

The captain's expression showed a slight scepticism.

"She must be, sir," he remarked, "if it requires the Navy to go after her...."

"I think I'd better put you in the picture, Captain. Yu-Malu, who is of Chinese extraction, has attempted to blackmail the British Government..." He gave a brief account of the Dragon Princess's activities. The captain listened in amazement but it was quite obvious that he was only half convinced.

"This island is her headquarters, sir?" he said.

Race nodded.

"Yes. She is holding my personal assistant, Miss Evans, a prisoner. There should also be a member of British Intelligence. I'm not very sanguine that either of them will be alive when we get there, but there's always a chance...."

"We're making all the speed we can, sir. The sea's like a mill-pond and there's no sign of any dirty weather. We should come in sight of this island before long, sir."

"Long—but how long?" Race couldn't keep his voice from sounding dismal.

Yu-Malu would not waste time on her return. The chance of finding Katrina alive was remote.

Her Highness Princess Yu-Malu was in a furious temper. It didn't show in her proud and lovely face except for a hard glint in her eyes and a slight tightening of the beautifully moulded jaw.

The result of her appointment with Race at the

Post Office Tower had been bad enough, but to this had been added a small series of annoyances that had culminated in her being unable to leave for her island headquarters when she intended.

The plane, which had been specially designed for her, and incorporated a number of innovations, which she had, herself, invented had suffered a minor mishap. It was nothing very serious but it involved delay while it was put right.

Luckily, at the farm which belonged to a member of the Triad, there was a mechanic, also of the Hung Brotherhood, who was capable of putting matters right.

"It will necessitate going to the garage in the town, your Highness," said the man.

"How long will it be before we can leave?" demanded Yu-Malu.

"It will take some time...."

"How long?" she repeated impatiently.

"I cannot tell exactly, your Highness," said the mechanic. "Tomorrow morning at the earliest. I shall work all night but I have no assistance. Because of that it will take longer...."

"Very well," said Yu-Malu. "I wish you to let me know the instant it is ready."

"Yes, your Highness."

Her host, who but for the slight almond shape to his eyes, would never have been taken for a Chinese, and indeed was believed in the surrounding district of Slavic origin, conducted her and the one remaining Dragonfly with her who had piloted the helicopter, into the farmhouse.

"If your Highness will honour my humble residence by partaking of a meal," he said with great deference, "I will prepare it with my own hands."

"You have as usual sent your staff away?" said the Dragon Princess, after graciously accepting.

"Of course, your Highness. Is it not one of our rules that when you come here, I arrange to be alone except for members of the Brotherhood."

He pushed forward a comfortable chair in the pleasantly furnished sitting room. Yu-Malu sat down with a smooth and graceful movement. The Dragonfly who had waited until she was seated found herself a chair.

"I shall bring you tea," said the host, with a low bow. "In the excellent tradition of our beloved country."

He went to the door and went out. They had held the conversation in Chinese. Yu-Malu helped herself to one of her tiny cigarettes.

"You are distressed that we have had to leave so many of our Dragonflies behind," she said when she had lighted the cigarette. "Is it not so?"

The Dragonfly moved uneasily.

"You read my thoughts, your Highness."

"Do not worry about them. They will not be harmed. I shall arrange to have them all safely brought back to us."

The girl smiled.

"I should have known that your Highness would not allow these British to keep them prisoners for long."

"My agents will find out where they have been taken

and then we can plan their escape. It will not be difficult."

She smoked for a while in silence. Her eyes had narrowed slightly as she concentrated her thoughts on the situation. This setback to her plans was due to Anthony Race.... Anthony Race should be made to suffer, first through Katrina and then in the most painful way she could devise....

The host came in with a tray on which was set out an exquisite teapot and bowl of the Hung-wu period.

"But this is lovely!" exclaimed Yu-Malu.

"Alas. It is all that is left, your Highness. I have treasured these pieces as my family treasured them before me."

"They are very, very beautiful."

"They are yours, if your Highness would deign to accept so humble a gift...."

"Keep them, they will remind you of the past glories of China and the glories that are to come. But I thank you all the same." She picked up the bowl of tea, which he had poured out and sipped it. "This is delicious."

"Your presence illumines the walls of my simple abode." He bowed low. "The humble meal I prepare for you will be ready in an hour."

Yu-Malu thanked him and when he had gone, returned to planning the very painful demise of Anthony Race.

* * * * * *

Police Constable Withers rode slowly down the

lane on his decrepit bicycle. Every now and again the ratchet on the free wheel slipped a cog but he was used to it. Visions of his supper floated like a mirage before his eyes as he pedalled along the rutted road.

In a few more minutes he would be off duty. He was on his way to report to the little police station and then he could hurry away to his small cottage and the supper, flanked by a pint of beer, which his buxom wife would have waiting for him.

He passed the gate that led up to the farm and then he saw, several yards ahead, a skulking figure disappearing through a gap in the hedge that lined the lane.

Police Constable Withers became suddenly alert.

Joe Higgs!

Withers increased his speed. Joe Higgs. Up to his tricks again. This time he'd get him!

Police Constable Withers got off his bicycle, leaned the machine against the hedge, and forced his large body through the gap in the hedge where he had seen the poacher vanish.

Beyond, as he knew, was a ragged wood that frayed out to the meadows belonging to the farm. Withers paused on the other side of the hedge and listened. Somewhere ahead he could hear the faint rustle of leaves and the crack of a broken branch under the foot of his quarry.

Withers crept forward cautiously, trying to move as quietly as his bulk would allow. In the excitement of the chase he had forgotten his supper. If he could catch Joe Higgs it would be a feather in his cap. Joe had always been too clever to be caught with any evidence on him. Perhaps this was going to be the exception.

There was a possibility, of course, that the poacher had seen him, but he was hoping that he hadn't. The light from his lamp on his bicycle was so dim with the smoke from the oil wick that it was scarcely visible. He had been going to clean it that morning but he thanked his stars that he had been prevented...

There was no sign of the poacher. No sound came from the thickly growing trees ahead. Withers frowned. Was he going to lose Joe Higgs again?

He moved cautiously forward for a few yards and then stopped again to listen.

No sound.

He went on again, moving slowly and pausing at frequent intervals. Presently the trees began to thin out and he found himself at the end of the copse with the meadow stretching, dark and deserted, in front of him.

But of Joe Higgs there wasn't a trace. He must have missed the poacher in the wood.

Withers cursed under his breath. All his trouble for nothing and he'd be late for his supper as well. He was turning to retrace his steps back to where he had left his bicycle when he saw something moving across the meadow.

Could it be Joe Higgs?

The meadow was bordered by trees and the moving shadow was going in the direction of the farthest line. Drawing a deep breath, Withers went in pursuit.

It was so dark that there was little risk of his being

seen. In fact it was all he could do to keep sight of the man, if it was a man, he was following. Several times he lost sight of that shadowy blot ahead and eventually he vanished.

But Withers had come so far that he determined to continue. He came at last to the line of trees that divided the meadow from a smaller field. There was a hedge and a ditch as well and the constable, who had forgotten about the ditch, nearly fell into it. But he managed to save himself by grabbing at the hedge with the result that he tore his hand on some sharp thorns. As he pulled himself up he caught sight of a light in the farther field.

It was a dim light and it was moving away from him. Gritting his teeth, Withers negotiated the ditch, dragged himself through the hedge, and paused to regain his breath.

Joe Higgs would be unlikely to give away his presence with a light. It must be someone connected with the farm. There was no point in going on. He might as well get back to his bicycle, ride to the police station, and go home.

And then he saw something that put all thought of Joe Higgs out of his mind, something that caused a thrill of excitement to stir his sluggish pulses.

In the middle of the field was a plane.

It was only shadowy but there was no doubt.

Police Constable Withers drew in his breath with a gasping hiss. Every police station in the country had received instructions to look out for a plane. Some foreign woman had escaped after a fight in that new tower place in London. Withers couldn't remember her name or what she was supposed to have done but he'd been instructed as a matter of routine to keep a look out for an unknown plane. He hadn't paid much attention at the time but here, in this field belonging to the farm, he'd stumbled on one.

He was neither very bright nor very intelligent but he realized that what he had found might be important. The best thing he could do would be to ride back to the police station as fast as he could and report the matter to the sergeant. It might mean promotion.

As quickly as he could he hurried across the meadow, through the strip of woodland, and out into the lane where he had left his bicycle.

Mounting the machine he pedalled off down the lane as fast as his sturdy legs would move...

The station sergeant, a grizzled man with a sour expression on his long face, looked up as Withers almost ran in the door.

"You're in a hurry," he growled. "What's chasin' yer?"

"The plane!" exclaimed Withers breathlessly. "It's the plane!"

The station sergeant glared at him suspiciously.

"What are you talkin' about? Chased by a plane?"

"It were in the field," gasped Withers. "Up at the farm."

"Have you been in 'The Feathers'?" demanded the sergeant.

"No, sir...."

"Then what d'you mean by bein' chased by a plane in a field?"

"I didn't say nothin' about bein' chased," asserted Withers indignantly. "It were you what said it."

"Me?" cried the sergeant turning a dusky shade of purple in his rage. "You must be either mad or drunk! I never said nothin' about bein' chased by a plane."

"You asked me what were chasin' me," said the constable.

"An' you said a plane," broke in the sergeant.

"I didn't mean that I were bein' chased by a plane," shouted Withers. "There were a plane in this 'ere field."

The sergeant became instantly alert.

"Why couldn't you have said that at once?" he asked wrathfully. "That's the plane we've been asked to look out for...."

"That's what I've been tryin' to tell you...."

"You want to learn to come straight to the point, me lad," grunted the sergeant. "You say there's a plane up at the farm?"

"Yes—in a field. It 'ad no right to be there."

"I'll get on to 'eadquarters," said the sergeant. "You'd better 'ang on."

"Can't I go an' get me supper?" asked Withers. Now that the first excitement had worn off he was feeling hungry again.

"No!" snapped the sergeant. "Not until I've got me instructions."

He got through to the police station in the nearby

town, which in turn got through to Scotland Yard.

The news caused great excitement in the august building. After a little delay, the sergeant was told to do nothing but hold himself in readiness with all the men he could muster until he heard further.

Since the only man he could muster was Police Constable Withers he ordered that unfortunate individual to wait for further instructions.

In the meanwhile, the Special Branch in London got really busy. Anthony Race was not available so they acted on heir own initiative. Forty men in police tenders, armed with tear gas bombs and issued with revolvers sped towards the farm at which Police Constable Withers had reported the presence of an unidentified plane.

"We'll show that fellow Race how these things should be handled," boasted the Chief Superintendent in charge of the operation.

Which was an unfortunate remark as events turned out.

* * * * * * *

Although she was seething with impatience at the delay, Yu-Malu with oriental stoicism made the best of it. It was one of those things that could not be helped.

She had no knowledge, while she sat and talked to her host and the Dragonflies about her plans for China, of the men who were racing towards the farm in the hope of effecting her capture. The man who patrolled the farm on the lookout for any intruders had failed to spot Police Constable Withers when he had made his momentous discovery.

"Although I am desolate that your journey should have been delayed, your Highness," said her host, "it has brought me great joy. To be privileged to talk with you and hear your plans for China is something that I shall cherish for the rest of my life. It has been most gracious of you to put up with my poor hospitality."

"You do yourself an injustice," responded Yu-Malu. "You have extended the true hospitality of your house to me and I am honoured by it. I am anxious to return to my island headquarters for reasons which I need not explain to one so gifted with intelligence as yourself, but I shall always look upon this period as a pleasant interlude in my eternal war against the Western world."

"Your graciousness is only exceeded by your tran-scendent beauty, your Highness." Her host bowed low. He did not sit in the presence of Yu-Malu. He would have considered it an insult. The Chinese have brought politeness to a fine art.

Yu-Malu was sipping tea made in the Chinese manner when the first hint of danger reached her. It came from the mechanic who had just come from the village.

"There are many men with cars crowding the streets, your Highness," he said. "They are on their way here...."

Yu-Malu rose quickly to her feet.

"The plane must have been seen and reported," she said. "We must be prepared for an attack."

"I have arms," said her host, "but, alas, few to use

them. In deference to your Highness I have sent my staff who are not of our order away...."

"Do not worry," said Yu-Malu, "there are sufficient of us to repel these scum who would lay their unclean hands upon us. There are also certain special appliances in the plane, which can be brought into use. Let us seek them at once and while there is time."

The mechanic led the way to the field, the others following him. Everything was quiet as yet. The plane, almost invisible in the darkness, loomed up above them. The steps were lowered and Yu-Malu climbed swiftly up into the fuselage. She called to the Dragonflies and they went up after her. From a compartment near the tail, the Dragon Princess took out three long shining tubes with a bulbous attachment at one end.

"Take these," she ordered. "The approach road must be covered."

The Dragonflies took the queer looking tubes and descended to the ground. Yu-Malu followed with a grey-painted box.

"What are those?" asked the mechanic curiously.

"We call them the Dreamless Sleep," answered Yu-Malu. "It is a special powder contained in these cartridges which on contact with the air turns into a gas. One slight breath of it will render a person completely senseless for a period of several hours." She was opening the box while she spoke. In it were dozens of green-coloured cylinders. "These fit into the breech of the tubes," she continued, "and are fired by compressed air. They burst on contact. There are enough here to put an army to sleep."

"Allow me to suggest the most strategic places, your Highness," ventured her host, "I am more familiar with the layout of the land than you."

"That is a wise suggestion," said Yu-Malu. "See to it. At the first sign of these men—fire the tubes."

The mechanic was following the Dragonflies and the owner of the farm but she stopped him.

"Remain here," she ordered.

"Yes, your Highness."

"This damaged part that we await—it will not prevent the plane taking off and flying?"

"No, your Highness, it will not do that. But there is danger that it may affect the safety of the plane. It is not so important in itself but it connects with a portion of the lubricating system...."

"We must take the risk," broke in Yu-Malu curtly. "Prepare the plane to leave as soon as possible."

The mechanic looked dubious

"It is a risk, your Highness."

"I'm used to risks. Do as I say."

"Very well, your Highness."

"Be as quick as you can. We may have to leave in a hurry."

Yu-Malu walked briskly away in search of the others. As she reached them she heard the sound of approaching car engines.

"They are coming, your Highness," muttered the owner of the farm.

"Get ready to fire. The Dreamless Sleep acts

instantly," said Yu-Malu.

From where they stood they could see the road that led down to the village. In the distance lights were visible—a necklace of lights that were strung out along the winding road. The sound of the approaching cars grew louder as they sped up the slight rise.

The Dragonflies tensed, their hands gripping the polished tubes. The box of cartridges lay open at their feet. Yu-Malu picked up several, ready to reload instantly. Her eyes were fixed on the road, watchful for the exact moment when she would give the order to release the stupefying gas.

The first of the string of cars topped the rise...

"Now!" snapped the Dragon Princess.

The tubes hissed viciously and the missiles sped towards their target. The first car swerved sharply. Two others crashed into it and one overturned.

Yu-Malu swiftly reloaded the tubes and again the gas shells sped silently through the darkness. Again and again the tubes were reloaded and fired and the cars piled up in a confused heap.

"That will do," said Yu-Malu. "Quickly now. Back to the plane."

"Had we not better make sure that these men are put out of action?"' asked her host.

"There is no need. It would be dangerous to go near them until the gas has dispersed. Come!"

They hurried back to the plane. The mechanic was busy refueling.

"How long?" asked the Dragon Princess.

"It will be ready to take off in half an hour, your Highness."

Yu-Malu ordered the Dragonflies to replace the tubes and the remainder of the cartridges.

"You will take something before you leave, your Highness?" asked the owner of the farm.

She shook her head.

"I am sorry to have brought this on you," she said. "You had better leave the farm at once, before you can be arrested. You will be well rewarded. The Hung will look after you...."

"Have no fear for me, your Highness. It is you who matter. I am worried that you should have to fly the plane in its present condition...."

"Nothing will happen to me," said Yu-Malu. "It is written in their stars that I shall survive to lead our beloved China to victory and dominate the world."

* * * * * * *

Night came down slowly on the island and with a slight wind that felt chill after the heat of the day. Katrina, perched uncomfortably in the tree-top refuge, suffered from violent cramp in her legs. She got a certain amount of relief by stretching them alternately, but this was a difficult job and once resulted in her nearly falling out of the fork in which she had wedged herself.

They were still searching for her down below. She could hear their chattering voices and see a myriad of small lights flickering like fireflies. She dared not come down for that would have meant almost certain capture. So long as she remained where she was she was fairly safc.

To add to her discomfort there were dozens of flying creatures who seemed to regard her as a heaven sent meal. They were larger than mosquitoes and their bites were painful. Her face and bare arms came up in lumps that irritated intensely.

She wondered how long she could endure it up here. Apart from her cramped limbs and the bites of the flying insects, she was ravenously hungry.

It was a clear night with a bright moon. From where she was perched she could, by craning her neck, see part of the airstrip. There were a number of moving lights on it, but Yu-Malu had not yet returned. She had neither seen nor heard any sign of the plane. It was pretty certain, she thought, that they would make desperate efforts to find her before the Dragon Princess got back.

Her eyes ached and the lids felt as though they had been weighted with lead. Once she fell asleep, felt herself falling, and jerked herself awake. She would have welcomed sleep if it hadn't been so dangerous....

The lights were strung out among the hills. She could see them there. It was only when they were close beneath her that the thick canopy of foliage shut out her view and she only relied on her ears.

It was all quiet immediately below and she wondered if she dared risk coming down out of the trees.

The spasms of cramp were getting worse and the

insects seemed to be increasing....

But once she was on the ground it would be difficult to keep hidden from the searchers. They would expect that she would be hiding in some of the caves or among the trees and they would keep on going over the same ground again until they found her....

She wondered how it would end. Would she die up here from hunger or would she fall out of the tree from sheer exhaustion?

What else was there? There was little chance of rescue....

Unless Anthony Race had received a message from Peter Dale...? But Dale did not know the location of the island. He couldn't know that—she didn't know. It might be anywhere—a small, oblong strip of land in the midst of an expanse of sea. Not a very easy place to find unless one knew in which sea to look—and even then....

Quite suddenly she heard a sound from below,

It was quite faint at first and she wondered what it was. It seemed to be coming nearer and her heart jumped! It was the sound of snapping twigs.

Somebody was climbing the tree.

Katrina held her breath and strained her cars. There was no doubt. A branch broke with a loud crack. With infinite caution, she peered down through a gap she had made in the matted foliage. But it was dark under the canopy of twining branches and thickly growing leaves and she could see nothing....

But the sound of the climber grew steadily closer.

A wave of panic swept over her. They had found her hiding place. There was nothing she could do. At any moment the climber would break through the screen of leaves and she was helpless to do anything about it. There was no way of concealing herself—up here above the mass of foliage....

She braced herself in the fork more firmly. At least she could put up a fight....

Nearer and nearer came the climber. She could hear the sound of quick, heavy breathing... With wide, fear darkened eyes, she stared at the green screen just below her. The tree was vibrating. She felt it shaking under her. How long would it be before the climber burst through that screen of leaves...?

Suddenly the leaves were thrust aside and she saw a hideous face and a large, misshapen head. A nightmare of a face with small, cruel eyes and a thick-lipped mouth. The tufts of black hair that grew on the great head hung down in straggling, greasy strands, and the seamed face was wet with sweat. Clenched between yellow teeth was a knife, long and thin.

He uttered an animal-like grunt as he saw her. A hand, small like a child's except for the swollen veins that stood out on the back, reached up and gripped the branch just below her. She shrank away, pressing herself farther into the fork, as he pulled himself up out of the concealing foliage.

He was a dwarf.

His great malformed head looked too big and heavy for the tiny body. But his strength must have been enormous for he drew himself up with one hand and held on to the branch while with the other hand he took the knife from between his teeth.

"Got you!" The voice was high-pitched and thin but the little eyes snapped viciously. "Got you!"

He slashed at her feet but the knife missed by an inch. He grunted and drew himself farther up, swinging the knife back for a second attempt.

Katrina drew up her legs sharply, fell backwards, and, before she could save herself, went crashing down through the leaves and branches towards the ground below.

CHAPTER TWELVE

It was still dark when Anthony Race awoke after a short rest and swung himself out of the bunk. The throb of the ship's engines was steady and rhythmic and he judged from the sound that they were still travelling at full speed.

The night was still fine but he could feel that slight lowering of the temperature that comes just before dawn. He made his way up to the bridge where he found the captain poring over a chart in the chart-house.

"How are we making out?" asked Race.

The captain pointed to the chart with the stem of his pipe.

"See that pencil dot there?" he said. "That's the island, according to my calculations." The pipe stem travelled down to another pencilled dot. "That's our present position. We ought to be within sight of the island in about six hours, sir."

"Good."

"Now," said the captain, straightening up, "what do we do when we get there?"

"We attack it. Open fire with all we've got...."

"What about the young lady, Miss Evans?"

Race frowned.

"Can we land some men under cover of the fire?" he asked.

The captain sucked at his pipe dubiously.

"We should have to send 'em in launches, sir," he answered. "We can't bring the ships in too close. It's probably rocky and surrounded with reefs...."

"We'll just have to do the best we can," said Race, after a pause. "The island must be destroyed—that's the main object. I very much doubt if Miss Evans is still alive, anyhow...."

"We'll spread out and surround the island," said the captain. "Do you know whether they've any sort of boat that they can try and get away in?"

"I know nothing about the place at all, except that it's this woman, Yu-Malu's headquarters. I should imagine there's quite a number of people there...."

"I suppose, if we can take the woman alive, you'd prefer it?"

"Naturally, but I'm not insisting on it," said Race. "All I want to make sure of is that she doesn't escape."

"We ought to be able to ensure that," said the captain. "If she can get away from us it'll be a miracle."

"Yu-Malu has a habit of pulling off miracles," said Race.

* * * * * * *

Katrina managed to partly check her fall by clutching at branches but even with this braking effect she landed with a bump that knocked what little breath she had left out of her. Her hands were torn and bleeding and her whole body was one huge, aching bruise.

From above her she could hear the cracking and slithering of the dwarf as he came down after her.

She tried to struggle up but she found that she was too weak...

There was no hope. When he got down she would be helpless, at his mercy. She suddenly felt sick....

And then she heard a loud cracking sound and a guttural cry. A shower of broken twigs and leaves fell on her, followed, quite close, by a heavy thud.

The dwarf must have fallen.

She held her breath, listening, but there was no other sound. Was he stunned? Or perhaps badly hurt? She crawled painfully over to where she had heard his body strike the ground. It was fairly dark, here, under the trees, but she managed to make out the huddled figure.

It lay face downwards, quite motionless, the great head twisted sideways. She could dimly see the distorted face and the small, staring eyes. He was motionless, not a breath disturbed the ugly body.

He must be dead. Had the fall broken his neck?

And then she saw the glint in the middle of a spreading stain between his shoulders. It was the tip of a knife. An inch of sharp steel....

He must have been holding the knife when he fell and the force of his fall had driven the sharp blade clean through his body....

Katrina breathed a prayer of thankfulness. But she wasn't safe yet! The searchers would still be looking for her. With difficulty she managed to get on her knees. She must find somewhere she could hide until she had recovered her strength....

Faintly in the distance came the sound of an engine. It grew rapidly louder and louder until it became a screaming roar....

Yu-Malu's plane.

The Dragon Princess had returned.

* * * * * * *

Sin Wu was waiting by the foot of the gangway steps as Yu-Malu descended from the plane in the underground cavern. His face was grave and troubled.

"Your Highness," he said bowing low, "I am filled with joy at your return but I have serious news that will displease you...."

"What has happened, Sin Wu?" she asked sharply.

"The woman, Katrina Evans, has managed to escape," replied Sin Wu, "she took advantage of an unforeseen accident to use your Highness's private lift and reach the open air...."

"She must be found," said Yu-Malu. "She must be still on the island. Has a search been made?"

"Search has been in progress throughout the night," said the old man. "Immediately I was told I issued orders that a search was to be carried out until she was found. Every available person is, even now, carrying out my orders."

"The girl has got to be found...."

"She will not last long without food, your Highness."

"I want her found and brought to me," ordered Yu-Malu curtly. "I am going to my apartment to bathe and change. Send my maid to me."

"It shall be done, even as you say, your Highness," answered Sin Wu. "I will accompany you, with your permission, and explain how this woman succeeded in escaping..."

"I see that nobody can be blamed," said Yu-Malu, when he had finished his explanation. "But the girl shall be severely punished.... It is very hot in these corridors. Has anything gone wrong with the air-conditioning plant?"

"I have noticed the alteration in temperature, your Highness," said Sin Wu. "The engineers have instructions to make a thorough examination of the plant.... Your negotiations were not successful, your Highness?"

"They were not!" snapped Yu-Malu. "It was a trap. I nearly fell into it. But I had taken precautions...."

"The people of the West do not attach so much value to the given word as we do," commented the old Chinaman. "I was afraid that you might not find it so easy as you imagined...."

"I have not finished, Sin Wu. They shall pay heavily. It will not only be their gold that I shall destroy. I shall crush them—like that."

She closed her hand tightly. Sin Wu regarded her with an expressionless face as he opened the door to her suite and stood aside for her to enter.

"I will send the maid to you, your Highness," he said and with a low bow left her.

Yu-Malu went straight to her private pool. Stripping off her clothes, she slid gratefully into the water, enjoying the sensual caress of the warm fluid flooding over the rounded curves of her perfect body.

Her maid came in and tidied away the clothes she had left on the side of the pool and brought a wrap for her to put on when she came out.

After swimming a few strokes, Yu-Malu let herself float lazily. Her plans had been thwarted, but only temporarily. She still had the power to strike a crippling blow, and she determined that this time the people of the West should have no alternative.

They should lose their gold, all of it, and when the entire financial structure was in chaos, she would step in with the gold she held. But this time her demands would be greater...

A soft-toned buzzer interrupted her thoughts.

"Switch on the speaker," she called to the maid and the girl depressed a switch. The voice of Sin Wu, harsh and unusually urgent, came over the concealed speaker.

"Your Highness, your highness! Ships have been sighted on the horizon—warships! They are steaming with all speed in this direction. There are many ships...."

"Say that I will speak with him in a moment," said Yu-Malu. "Switch the microphone through."

She swam to the side of the pool and stepped out, her golden body sending a shower of water that glistened in the light. She picked up the absorbent wrap and draped it over her shoulders. In her bare feet she went swiftly to the table by the chair at the other end of the pool.

"You are there, Sin Wu?" she said.

"I am here, your Highness."

"Listen then. Have the force field ready. Then come to me."

"It shall be done, your Highness."

Yu-Malu turned to the waiting maid.

"I shall require a suit, the plain black. See that it is ready."

"Shall I not dry you, your Highness?"

"I will dry myself. Go quickly, there is no time to lose."

The Chinese girl bowed and hurried away to the bedroom. She opened the huge wardrobe and selected the dress that her mistress had described, laid it on the bed, and fetched underclothes, stockings and shoes.

Yu-Malu joined her just as she had finished getting the clothes ready. With the deft assistance of the maid, the Dragon Princess dressed.

The maid was doing her hair when Sin Wu arrived.

"How long will it be before these ships are within range?" asked Yu-Malu.

"An hour and a half, perhaps two hours, your Highness," answered the old man.

"The detonating ray will account for them," said Yu-Malu calmly. "Their ammunition magazines will explode as soon as they get within its range. This is the result of the message that the man, Dale, succeeded in sending...."

"He couldn't have known the position of the island,

your Highness...."

"They must have worked that out for themselves. It will do them no good. They will be blown to pieces...."

A violent tremor shook the room. The priceless carvings and china rattled and a vase fell with a thud on the soft carpet.

"What was that?" demanded Yu-Malu.

"There have been many tremors recently, your Highness. The subterranean forces that originally produced this island are, I fear, once more becoming active...."

"Sound the alarm calling everyone to the conference room—even those who are searching for the girl, Evans. Order the plane in the lower cavern to be fueled and prepared...."

"Your Highness is wise," murmured Sin Wu. He bowed and withdrew. Yu-Malu turned to the frightened maid.

"Pack a few things in a suitcase," she said curtly.

"Yes, your Highness."

"Take it to the lower cavern and wait there for me." She patted the girl on the arm. "Don't be frightened, child. You will not be left."

A loud, but musical note sounded like a golden trumpet. It rang through the corridors, penetrating every room and corner of the underground headquarters, calling all those who lived and worked there, to the conference room.

Katrina, crouching in a shallow hole in the rocks near the coast, heard a similar trumpet-like note ring out over the island, and wondered what it could be.

She was wet with spray from the sea, and stiff and sore from the scratches and cuts she had suffered during her fall from the tree.

With great pain and difficulty she had managed to crawl to this hiding place, keeping in the concealment of the undergrowth. Twice, during the nightmare journey, she had almost fallen into the hands of the searchers. They had come so close that a few steps nearer and they would have trodden on her. But she lay still, not daring to breath, until they had moved away.

But there was more than the proximity of the searchers to frighten her. There had been more earth tremors and the last had been more severe than any that had gone before. It had sent a great rock crashing into the sea and nearly scared her to death.

Had she gone through all she had only to be engulfed in an earthquake. It could only be some kind of underground upheaval that could have caused the severe tremors. And yet the island and its surrounding looked peaceful enough. The dawn had broken serenely and now the sun was shining in a cloudless sky, its warmth beating down pleasantly.

The trumpet note was still filling the air and she could hear faintly the sound of excited voices somewhere farther inland. It must be some kind of signal or alarm, she thought. Perhaps it was to call off the search for her.

There was no other sound anywhere except the sea gently breaking over the rocks, and she ventured to look out of her hiding place. The creamy surf ebbed and flowed among the rocks and, beyond them, lay an expanse of limpid blue, splashed with silver where the sun struck the ripples of tiny waves.

And suddenly she felt her heart leap. Away on the horizon she could see a number of dark shapes, small, toy-like shapes, but unmistakable....

Ships.

With straining eyes she watched. There were a number of them, grouped in a kind of formation. Were they just passing? Or had Peter Dale's message brought them?

Katrina watched them until the glare on the water hurt her eyes. They seemed to be getting nearer but that might be an illusion. She could only wait and—hope.

* * * * * * *

"There's your island," said the captain, handing his binoculars to Race. "We're dead on! Not bad, eh?"

Race stared through the glasses. A brownish, oblong shape with a hint of green, it lay low in the sea, neither very large nor very conspicuous.

"Not very impressive," remarked the captain. "Easily miss it if you weren't looking for it."

"How long before we reach it?" asked Race, handing the binoculars back.

"About an hour. Guns are loaded and the gunners at their posts. We'll open fire with a broadside of fourteen inchers—from both directions! That ought to make 'em sit up."

"And then?"

"If there's much left of it, sir, after we've finished shelling it, we can send a landing party to clear up the debris. That's what we agreed, sir."

"Well, I've changed my mind, captain."

Race helped himself to a cigarette and lit it.

"You had it all worked out, eh?"

"Yes, sir," said the captain. "We like everything cut and dried in the Navy...."

"Well, we're not going to do it quite that way," broke in Race.

Astonishment swept across the captain's face like a breaking wave. He had been sure that Race would have no fault to find with his plan of operations.

"I don't understand," he began.

"I think," said Race, "that I was placed in charge of this expedition. Is that right?"

"Yes, of course...."

"Then I should prefer you to do it my way. Please signal to the flotilla to stop."

"To stop?" exclaimed the incredulous captain.

"To stop and drop anchor," said Race. "I cannot imagine that Yu-Malu has left herself exposed to an attack from the sea without some kind of precaution. We know her inventive genius. I've no wish to lose these ships...."

"How can we lose 'em?" demanded the captain. "Mines, d'you mean?"

Race shook his head.

"Nothing so crude," he said. "Possibly there are some kind of mines. I am thinking more of an electronic device. A woman who could invent a machine for the destruction of gold would have little difficulty in destroying—ships!"

"Good God!" exclaimed the captain. "Are you serious?"

"Very serious."

"What do you propose to do, then?"

"I propose to approach the island by launch. With a selected party we can possibly land and find out exactly what these headquarters of Yu-Malu are like."

The captain pursed his lips doubtfully.

"It's risky," he began but Race interrupted him.

"It's a risk that I must take," he said firmly. "I want to find Katrina Evans if I can. When we start shelling the place she could become a victim to our own guns. If that can be prevented...."

"But that means penetrating into the heart of the place," said the captain. "If you're caught...."

"Then you'll have to go ahead and bombard the place. Don't consider us. In all probability we shan't be alive."

The captain was reluctant but he carried out the orders. A radio signal was sent in code to the other ships of the flotilla to stop and drop anchor and a fast launch was lowered from the destroyer.

Into this Race, with a handful of picked men, took with him a portable two-way radio, rifles, hand grenades, and a couple of machine-guns. The man at the wheel started the powerful engine and, with the captain's 'good luck' ringing in their ears, they glided away from the hull of the destroyer and swept round in a wide circle, heading in the direction of the distant island.

Race sat in the prow of the launch, spray forming two wings on either side of him, thrown up in huge arcs as the speeding boat cut through the swelling sea.

The island was almost invisible from the launch and he was hoping that they would be invisible from the island. If the flotilla had been seen it was probable that the smaller launch might pass unnoticed. It could also pass under any electronic ray that might be in force, much in the same way that low-flying planes dodged the enemies radar.

If they could land without being seen there was a chance, a slim one, that they might find Katrina. It was more than likely that she was dead. At the same time, Yu-Malu might realize that Katrina would be more useful to her alive—as a hostage. That was what Race had hoped, and still hoped.

The launch sped through the sea, rapidly decreasing the distance between it and the island. Through his glasses Race could make it out more plainly now—a low, rock-girt piece of land with uneven crest of tree-clad hills. The white spume of the breaking waves against the rocks showed dearly, and he sought for a break in the white foam that would indicate a channel through which they could ease the launch and effect a landing.

But there was nothing of the kind.

The island appeared to be completely hemmed in by rocks. There was a possibility that there would be better facilities for landing on the other side.

He suggested this to the helmsman. The launch veered and headed towards one end of the island. They rounded the point, drawing in nearer to the shore, and slowing down a little.

The line of white breakers seemed at first to be as unbroken as the other side of the island, but presently Race made out a narrow inlet in the line of creaming surf. It was very narrow. From that distance away it looked too small to admit the launch but he decided to risk it.

As the man at the wheel reduced speed still more and turned the prow of the launch towards the little break in the rocks, Race heard a low, muttering sound like that of distant thunder. He glanced up at the sky but it was clear. It couldn't have been thunder. What was it?

Again it came, a menacing rumble that shook the air round them. It must come from the island.

"Did you hear that?" asked Race.

The helmsman nodded.

"Yes, sir."

"What do you make of it?"

The man shrugged his shoulders.

"Sounded like some kind of underground blasting operations, sir."

Race nodded. Perhaps that was it. The people of the

island were making some kind of alterations to their stronghold.

Very slowly, taking soundings for hidden reefs at almost every dozen yards, the launch crept cautiously towards the narrow break in the rocky coast.

As they drew nearer they could see that it was wider than it had looked at first glance. There was room and to spare for the launch. Beyond the piled rocks that formed each side was just visible a strip of sandy beach—an ideal landing spot if they could run the launch in safely....

* * * * * * *

Katrina did not see the launch approaching. Her eyes had got so painful from the glare of the sun on the sea that she had been forced to turn away and rest them by looking inland. When she looked again the ships in the distance had not got any nearer. She concluded that they must just be passing on the horizon although they didn't appear to be moving.

But this might be an optical illusion due to the strain on her eyes.

Sick with disappointment she stretched her tired and aching body in the shallow cave in which she lay concealed and in a few minutes she had drifted into a fitful sleep.

She was quite unaware that Anthony Race was preparing to set off for the island and soon would be making a landing on the other side.

She sank into a deeper sleep as exhausted nature

took control and began to repair the ravages of terror and physical exhaustion that had worn her out....

* * * * * *

The prow of the launch grounded softly in the soft sand. The helmsman had stopped the engine as they began to glide between the rocks and the boat covered the last few yards under its own momentum. So expertly had he judged it that there was no need to reverse his engine to stop.

As the boat came to a stop a sailor sprang ashore with a rope and held the launch in while the others joined him. The rope was made fast to a ringed spike driven into the sand and they took stock of their surroundings.

They had landed in a small, sheltered bay, hemmed in on three sides by rocks, those at the back, facing them, rising to a cliff, those on each side sloping up to join the escarpment. The beach was barely fifty yards wide and roughly the same depth.

Of the island they could see nothing at all. The high rocks blotted out any sign of it.

Race stood looking quickly about. The cliff at the back was sheer and, although there were piles of fallen rocks, it didn't look climbable. But the slopes at the side appeared more possible.

Armed with machine guns, Race and four of the crew began to climb the right hand slope. Although it was not so impossible as the cliff it was heavy going. There was a loose surface of small and crumbling-rock that made it difficult to maintain a foothold. Several times they slipped and slithered and almost fell.

They were a, good part of the way up when again there came that rumbling sound like thunder. This time they could locate it. It came from somewhere beneath the island. It was like a heavy explosion that shook the rock around them. A portion of the cliff top broke away and fell with a crash.

Race stopped, wiping his forehead with the back of his hand.

"I don't like the sound of this," he said.

"What do you think it is, sir?" asked one of the sailors.

"Some kind of volcanic action," answered Race.

"Could it be dangerous, sir?"

"It could be."

"Do we go on, sir?"

"Yes. It may only be a tremor...."

He had scarcely got the words out when there was a further thunderous rumbling, This time it was heavier and lasted longer. More of the cliff top fell with a resounding crash and one of the rocks near them split and toppled down to the sandy beach.

The whole earth was shaking.

"I don't think we'd better risk going any farther," said Race. "This looks as if it might be serious."

Gingerly they began to retrace their steps down the rocky slope. Slithering and sliding on the loose surface they eventually almost fell on to the beach.

The helmsman, who had been left on the launch, saw them coming and started his engine. Quickly they tumbled on board, the last man casting off. The launch, its engine reversed, moved out stem first through the rocky inlet. As they turned round to head back to the ships they saw the whole escarpment crumble and fall with a roar and a great cloud of dust, almost filling the sandy beach with the debris.

"Lucky we left when we did," muttered Race.

He wondered what was happening to the rest of the island.

* * * * * * *

Yu-Malu faced her followers in the crowded conference room and there was no sign in the calm loveliness of her appearance to indicate the bitterness in her heart. In this moment of defeat, when all her cherished dreams were crumbling to dust around her, she looked more like a conquering queen than a defeated princess. In her low, musical voice, she addressed the silent gathering.

"I am sad at what I have to say. We are beset, not only by the forces of man, but by the more powerful forces of nature. This island is the result of volcanic activity, as some of you know. The engineers who constructed these headquarters, where we have lived for so long, were under the impression that the volcanic forces that spawned this island in the middle of the sea were extinct. They were only sleeping.

"There are signs that at any moment, even while I stand here speaking to you, those forces which gave birth to this island will destroy it. Already cracks arc appearing in the lower corridors and the instruments in our laboratories register a tremendous upheaval in the bowels of the earth beneath us.

"At the same time a contingent of British warships are speeding towards us. I might have dealt with them, but against this greater danger I am powerless."

She looked round at the sea of faces before her. There was no sign of panic. They were as calm as she was herself.

"The saddest thing I have to tell you is that I cannot take you with me when I leave. But you have all been dedicated to our great cause and trained to take whatever fate shall overtake you with true Eastern fatalism. You have served me well and faithfully and your efforts have not been in vain. My plans have been thwarted this time, but I shall never falter in my avowed intention to bring the Western world to its knees and raise our beloved China to supreme and glorious power."

She had scarcely finished speaking when the whole room shook. The floor split across in a wide crack and a portion of the ceiling fell with a loud crash.

"Your Highness, there is no time to lose!" Sin Wu came forward urgently. "You must hurry or it will be too late."

Yu-Malu looked at the assembly, at the Dragonflies in all their young beauty, at the Chinese staff, the engineers and electricians, at all who had, as true members of the Hung Brotherhood, taken the oath of allegiance to her cause. Nothing could save them.

"Your Highness, come quickly!"

The claw-like hand of the old Chinese caught at her arm. She murmured a farewell and followed him out of the conference room.

The ground below them was trembling and the air of the corridor was tinged with an acrid, sulphurous smell. A distant explosion shook the place and there was the sound of breaking glass.

They hurried through the labyrinth of corridors. The air was hot and stifling. More explosions reached them but they kept on until they came to a heavy iron door set in a wall at the end of one of the wide passages.

"Those who are going with me are already waiting in the lower cavern?" said Yu-Malu.

"Yes, your Highness." Sin Wu took a key from his pocket and inserted it in the lock of the iron door. "I trust that the airlock mechanism has not been damaged by this subterranean activity."

"Have no fear," answered the Dragon Princess. "We shall not be harmed. The gods have not yet willed that we should join our ancestors."

The old man opened the door. Inside was a narrow flight of steps that led downwards.

"It is a pity that we cannot take the gold," said Yu-Malu bitterly. "Or the disintegrating machine. So much must be left behind."

"If the gold cannot belong to China it will belong to no other country," said the old man, as he descended the steps. "It will go back to the earth from which it was taken."

The steps were steep and long. Sin Wu went first

with Yu-Malu close behind him....

Back in the conference room those who had been left were silent. Their faces were white but resigned.

"It would be better, perhaps, to try and reach the open air?" suggested one of the engineers.

"We can but try," said an electrician.

"The lift in the cavern. It would take us all," suggested one of the Dragonflies.

They hurried out of the conference room. The corridor outside was full of fumes and even as they started to run along it a great fissure opened in the floor and a burst of flame shot up to the roof. The glass of the tanks lining the walls cracked and the water began to pour through.

"The other way!" shouted one of the electricians. "Past the laboratories."

They turned, fleeing into a branch passage that opened off the main corridor. But there was a great roar as they did so and a spout of molten rock and cinders filled the passage as one wall collapsed bringing down with if part of the roof. The molten rock, white-hot, and giving off a tremendous heat as it belched from a wide gap in the floor, began to roll sluggishly along towards them, lighting up their faces with a lurid glare.

"Back—get back!" cried one of the men. "There's no chance that way."

Stumbling and gasping from the fumes that filled the air, they ran back the way they had come, passing the open door of the conference room and on towards Yu-Malu's private apartments.

"Her Highness's private lift!" cried a frightened Dragonfly.

A tremendous explosion from somewhere in the heart of the underground headquarters shook the whole place and the lights went out.

"The generating plant," exclaimed an electrician.

In spite of their stoicism panic was beginning to overtake them. The Dragonflies were sobbing and whimpering, the sweat pouring down their lovely faces, as much from fear as from the intense heat, which was getting unbearable. There was another great crash of falling rock and stone. The entrance to the Dragon Princess's suite bulged outwards as a huge mass of glowing lava, a red-hot wall of liquid fire, breast high, came surging along the corridor. A great, hairy spider, released from behind the glass cage in which it had lived as the glass shattered, scuttled towards them but was shrivelled by the rapidly advancing lava.

Falling over each other in their hurry to get away from the advancing flood, they sought another passage, but the floor had already caved in and the walls were toppling. Wherever they went it was the same and the air was getting unbreathable from the sulphur fumes.

Coughing to ease their tortured lungs, and dizzy from the acrid smoke that swirled around them, they tried desperately to find a way out of the terrible, fiery trap in which they were caught.

But there was no way.

A sea of molten rock was filling the corridors, spewed up through the gaping holes in the floors, and into this huge fragments from the falling roof fell and became engulfed. As the skin on their bodies and faces began to blister from the heat, their screams of agony rose above the now almost continuous explosions. Faced by a white-hot wall of liquid rock and threatened by another that was moving slowly towards them from the rear, they clung together in their last despairing agony, screaming and crying in pain and fear and terror....

The two streams, glowing and steaming, met and mingled, and were joined by a third stream—a stream of molten gold from the stocks which Yu-Malu had gone to such trouble to accumulate.

* * * * * *

Yu-Malu and Sin Wu reached the lower cavern at last. It lay at the end of a long, natural passage in the rock, which ran from the foot of the flight of steps beyond the iron door.

The cavern was a large cave hewn out of solid rock, and water dripped from the wet roof. Although they could feel the shock of the volcanic eruptions that were taking place in the centre of the underground head-quarters, this part of the island ran under a spit of rock that projected out into the sea. The full force of the subterranean upheaval had not yet reached it.

On a platform of rock stood a strange looking object. It was the shape of a submarine but unlike any known design. It faced a great steel door that shut off the entrance to the cavern, resting on large rubber tyred wheels.

Near this unusual machine stood Yu-Malu's maid and ten Dragonflies.

"If you are ready, your Highness," said the old Chinese, "we will prepare to leave. There is no knowing how long it will be before the holocaust reaches us here."

"I am ready," said Yu-Malu. "Open the hatches, D.20."

One of the Dragonflies climbed up a short aluminium ladder that hung down from the side of the cigar-shaped machine and unfastened a sliding door in the hull.

"Set in motion the machinery for flooding the cavern, Sin Wu," ordered the Dragon Princess, as she mounted the ladder. "Bring up my suitcase."

The maid obeyed. The Dragonfly who had opened the sliding door in the hull had already gone inside. Yu-Malu watched as Sin Wu turned a switch set in the rock and water began to pour into the cavern from sluices in the steel door covering the entrance....

"It's as well that I had the foresight to make this mechanism independent of the main electric supply," said Yu-Malu. She motioned to the group of Dragonflies to enter the object. "I shall go inside, you will follow me," she turned to the waiting maid, "then you D.21." The Dragonfly still waiting on the rocky platform bowed. "As soon as we are inside, Sin Wu, you will set the time switch for the rising of the door, switch it on, and join us within. Is that clear?"

"Yes, your Highness," said the old man.

Yu-Malu stepped through the open door into the

machine. Her maid followed her quickly with the suitcase. A few seconds later D.21 mounted the ladder and entered.

Sin Wu adjusted the hand on a dial above the switch that had actuated the sluices and pulled down a second switch. Then he came over to the ladder and climbed into the strange machine. The ladder was pulled in by the Dragonfly who had entered first, the door was slid shut and fastened by bolts.

The inside of the machine was rather like the cabin of a plane except that the small windows were of thick glass and of a round shape, like the portholes of a ship. Up near the front, in the nose, was a complicated system of dials and levers and a wheel, again similar to the controls of a plane.

Yu-Malu took her seat in one of the padded chairs and two Dragonflies seated themselves in front of the controls. Sin Wu took the seat behind the Dragon Princess. The Chinese maid settled herself behind him. The others were already seated.

The cavern was already half full of water.

"It will not be long, your Highness," said the old man. "We shall go to the headquarters in the Amazon?"

"Yes," said Yu-Malu. "From there I shall continue my campaign against the West."

"It is a suitable place, your Highness," agreed the old Chinese folding his hands in his lap. "In those unexplored regions of that great river we should find the peace which is necessary for all imaginative undertakings...."

There was an explosion from the direction of the passage leading to the cavern and the water, now nearly to the roof, boiled up into a great wave.

"We have little time," said Sin Wu. "Let us pray that the volcanic upheavals will not reach us before the water gate is open."

The machine was floating easily in the water, keeping level and not tending to rise to the roof of the cavern. A steady hum filled the interior as one of the Dragonflies started the electric motors that were driven by storage batteries.

The water in the cavern rose higher and higher until it filled the whole of the cave. The steel door began to rise gently as the time switch came into operation.

Beyond was the seabed, lit faintly by the daylight percolating through the water. Among the weeds and the rocks, fish swam lazily, staring at them with curious eyes. To judge by the light, which was very dim, the sea was quite deep here.

"Are you ready, your Highness?" asked the Dragonfly at the controls of the strange craft.

"Yes, let us go," said the Dragon Princess.

The girl pulled forward a lever and the wheels on which the machine had stood before the cavern was flooded, slowly retracted into the hull. The sound of the engines increased, and was followed by a gurgling swish of water as the gears were engaged and the propellers, concealed within the hull, began to revolve.

Gently they moved forward, out into the sea. A series of muffled explosions reached them and the water swirled and grew turbid as the sandy bottom was stirred up in clouds.

"The island is doomed," said Sin Wu sorrowfully, "And those who were forced to stay behind will be sacrificed for the greatness of China."

"They will not have died in vain, Sin Wu," said Yu-Malu, "The glory of China will shine over the whole world. I swear it by all the gods of Cathay."

Her eyes gleamed with a fanatical light. Ruthless and lawless in her methods she might be, but she believed in her cause with all the force and power of a religion.

The machine moved forward with gathering speed, slipping through the water almost silently. It was the product of Yu-Malu's inventive genius, assisted by the two girls at the controls. She, who left nothing to chance if it could be avoided, had evolved this amazing machine for just such a purpose as it was at present being used.

"Keep at the lowest possible depth," she said. "We shall pass under the ships which have come to destroy us. If the detonating ray is still in force they will be destroyed but it may have been put out of action."

"Yes, your Highness."

The long, graceful craft, like a great silver fish, headed at full speed for the open sea....

* * * * * * *

Anthony Race, binoculars in hand, stood beside the captain on the bridge of the destroyer. The flotilla had come to a stop. The island was so close that Race could see it clearly without the aid of the glasses he carried.

There was a smoke haze hanging over it, like a great yellow-black veil, and the sea along the coastline was boiling among the craggy rocks in heavy breakers.

"What do you make of that?" he asked the captain.

"Looks as if the place was on fire,'" answered the captain.

Race frowned. Was Yu-Malu, in her desperation, going to destroy the place herself?

The captain was issuing orders to the radio operator. A warship had swung round so that she was broadside on to the island and a second later her twelve inch guns thundered and a salvo of high explosive shells screamed over the island.

Whether they burst or not, Race never knew. Obviously they must have, but the sound of their explosions was drowned by a far greater one.

The entire centre of the island seemed to split asunder with a deafening roar that put the thunder of the guns to shame. A huge spout of yellow, white, and orange flame shot up into the blue sky to a height that must have been nearly a thousand feet. With the flame went a thick column of black and yellow smoke that mushroomed out to an oil canopy that spread like a pall over the sky, blotting out the sun, its lower side tinged luridly by the fierce light of the roaring flame. Trees and rocks, flung into the air by the tremendous force of the eruption, fell like giant hail, crashing and rolling down the slopes of the hills. Masses of white-hot molten lava hurried through the smoke. Some fell in the sea with a great hiss of steam.

A huge fissure rent the island from end to end, belching forth fire and spewing up rivers of molten rock that ran in glowing streams everywhere, burning up the undergrowth and everything else in its path.

A gale-force wind, hot as though blowing from the gates of Hell, and thick with choking sulphur fumes, buffeted the ships and set the crews coughing violently. Burning cinders fell in showers on the decks and in the sea, sounding like heavy rain.

"My God!" muttered Race between his teeth. "There'll be nothing left of the island...."

"Nature has done a better job than we could, sir," said the captain.

A tidal wave, its crest whipped to cream by the wind, came sweeping towards them, breaking against the sides of the ships and smothering the decks and bridge with spray.

The captain wiping his eyes, picked up the engine room telegraph.

"We'll stand a little further off shore," he said, and was interrupted by the second officer.

"There's something in the sea, sir," he cried. "Look! There, can you see it? By God, it's a body...."

The captain grabbed the binoculars from Race.

"It's a woman," he exclaimed. "The wave must've carried her with it. Lucky she wasn't dashed against the side of the ship. She's probably dead, but we'd better try and get her out...."

He issued a string of orders. A seaman went over

the side with a lifebelt attached to a line. They watched him as he fought his way towards the dark speck that was tossing in the turbulent sea. He reached it and, with difficulty, succeeded in getting the lifebelt round the limp form.

He signalled to be hauled up, clinging to the line as it was slowly pulled in with its double burden.

Race and the captain had hurried down from the bridge to the rail as eager hands helped the rescued and rescuer aboard.

"She's nearly naked," grunted the captain. "Doesn't look to me as if there was any life in her...."

Anthony Race took one look at the white, drawn face.

"It's Katrina—Katrina Evans," he exclaimed. "Get the doctor, quickly...."

The heavy sound of further explosions from the island shook the air as the doctor made his examination.

"She's not dead," he announced, "but it's touch and go. Get her to a cabin with plenty of warm blankets and some hot coffee, strong and black..."

A tremendous shock sent a tremor through the whole ship. Race turned quickly from Katrina and looked in the direction of the island. It was sinking into the boiling sea amid clouds of hissing steam and smoke. Slowly, like a giant amphibian reptile, it settled lower and lower, huge waves breaking over it and almost instantly turning to steam as they touched the white-hot lava....

"I've never seen an island disappear before, sir," remarked the captain. "It's quite an experience."

Race said nothing. He was watching anxiously as Katrina was covered with a blanket and lifted gently on to a stretcher.

"Can I do anything?" he asked.

The doctor shook his head.

"All she needs is warmth and rest," he said. "She's suffering from exposure and shock. I'll give her an injection as soon as we get her snugly tucked up in a bunk."

The captain, who had been peering at the island through his glasses, lowered them, and turned to Race.

"Well, that's that," he said calmly. "That's the last you'll see of your Dragon Princess. Nobody could have survived that little lot unless they can perform a miracle."

Anthony Race stared thoughtfully at the inferno of swirling water, which was all that could be seen where the island had been.

"Remember I told you she has a habit of pulling off miracles," he answered seriously.

* * * * * * *

"It is safe to take it up now, D.20," said Yu-Malu.

"Yes, your Highness." The girl at the controls spoke to her companion. "Stand by to cut engines."

The nose of the machine tilted upward. D.20 watched the needle of a dial in front of her move slowly round.

"Extend wings, rudder and tail," she ordered.

D.21 pulled forward two levers. The machine gave a sudden upward leap.

"Open jet nozzles and fire jets."

The girl pulled forward a third lever. There was an answering roar from the rear of the machine. The hull quivered, vibrating under the powerful thrust of the twin jets. Sunlight flooded through the porthole windows as it leapt out of the sea and soared up into the clear blue of the sky, borne aloft on the swept-back wings that gave it the appearance of a swallow in flight.

"A remarkable invention, your Highness," said Sin Wu, approvingly as he looked out of the window and down at the sunlit sea, now far below them. "I do not think that the Western world possesses such a machine."

"You are right, Sin Wu," answered Yu-Malu. "This sub-aquaplane is the first of its kind. A fleet of them would be invaluable. It was partly for this that I wanted the cold fuel formula."

"It has enabled us to leave the island," said the old man. "Without this machine it would not have been possible. An ordinary plane would have been shot down by the anti-aircraft guns on the ships."

"We have got away," said Yu-Malu, "but we have had to leave a great deal behind. Some of our best scientific discoveries and the gold...."

"There will be more discoveries and more gold," said Sin Wu, philosophically. "The past is dead, the future as yet unborn, It is only in the present that we live."

"You speak wisdom, Sin Wu," she said. "But the future must be planned for and that is what the present is for."

The sub-aquaplane soared up until the sea beneath was lost in a haze, soared up until it was a speck in a limitless firmament of blue.

And, suddenly, Yu-Malu laughed, and laughed and laughed....

ABOUT THE AUTHOR

GERALD VERNER (1897-1980) was born John Robert Stuart Pringle in London on 31 January 1897, He was one of the most prolific and successful British writers of detective thrillers. His earliest novels, beginning in the late 1920s, were issued under the pen name of Donald Stuart, particularly his numerous "Sexton Blake" stories. His first novel as Gerald Verner. *THE EMBANKMENT MURDER*, appeared in 1933, and thereafter Verner became his adopted name, and was used for most of his work, although he continued to write occasionally as Stuart, also adding two other successful pen names, Derwent Steele and Nigel Vane. He published more than 120 novels, and was translated into over 35 languages. Many of his books were adapted into radio serials, stage plays, and films. He also wrote television serials, and one of his original screenplays, *DOUBLE DANGER*, was used for a 1961 episode of *THE AVENGERS*.

One of his most successful characters was Mr. Robert Budd, a Detective Superintendent of the C.I.D. Rather portly, deceptively sleepy-eyed, and seemingly a plodder, Mr. Budd was actually razor-sharp, and solved cases as well as any slick private detective of fiction. He was aided, rather unwillingly at times, by the melancholy and slower-witted Sergeant Leek, the butt of Mr. Budd's biting sarcasm.

Verner's work was frequently compared to that of Edgar Wallace, and he was noted for his exciting, fast-action plots, some of them recognised as classics of the locked-room and "impossible crime" genres.

www.ingramcontent.com/pod-product-compliance
Lightning Source LLC
Chambersburg PA
CBHW031429250626
47155CB00004B/1677